Opie Percival Read

On the Suwanee River

A Romance

Opie Percival Read

On the Suwanee River
A Romance

ISBN/EAN: 9783337249663

Printed in Europe, USA, Canada, Australia, Japan

Cover: Foto ©Andreas Hilbeck / pixelio.de

More available books at **www.hansebooks.com**

On the Suwanee River

A ROMANCE

BY

OPIE READ

Author of "The Carpetbagger," "Old Ebenezer," "The Jucklins,"
"My Young Master," "A Tennessee Judge," "Len Gansett,"
"A Kentucky Colonel," "The Wives of the Prophet,"
"The Tear in the Cup and Other Stories,"
"The Colossus," "Emmett Bonlore."

CHICAGO
LAIRD & LEE, PUBLISHERS

ON THE SUWANEE RIVER

CHAPTER I.

The Commodore's speculations in land were mostly imaginary; his surroundings were largely fanciful. And who so environed could have been practical? Who could have sat strong and business-like above dreamy addition, museful multiplication and the subtractions of revery? A few rods away, in front of the small white building wherein the Commodore sat and waited for buyers, flowed the Suwanee river, and to the right and the left, languid in the shade of the live oak, lay the village of Gaeta. A scene may be described, but a condition must be felt, and this place is a condition—atmosphere of velvet, silken breeze. Here nature has softened her accents, yellowed the clouds which elsewhere would be black, and the bird which flew from the north to escape the cold forgot his harsher notes. When the air was so still that the Spanish moss

hung motionless, the faint roar of a railway train
could be heard far away;—the low rumble of the
nineteenth century echoing.

And the Commodore sat and waited. He grew
weary of doing all the waiting himself, so he ad-
vertised for an assistant, declared through the
stagnant columns of a listless newspaper that he
wanted some one to help him. The Commodore
was a man of medium size, dark of countenance
and with a pretense of fierceness in his glance.
He boasted that he must have descended from a
family of pirates. He decorated himself with
the title of Commodore. He said that he had
commanded a fleet of blockade runners during
the war. It was known, confidentially, that he
had been captain and crew of a two-oar ferry
boat away up somewhere on the Tennessee river,
and that he had turned loose his property and let
it drift off when a rival ferryman had made it hot
by firing on him. His name was Hoke Adams.

The Commodore was sitting in his office one
morning about three weeks after the advertisement had appeared, when a young woman stepped
upon the doorsill and tapped like a bird.

" Walk right in, miss," exclaimed the Commodore, rolling out of his chair as if it were his intention to fall on the floor. But he caught him-

self, and not ungracefully. "Have this chair; sheepskin; easiest one in this restful community."

The young woman did not sit down. She stood with one hand resting on the top of a tall desk.

"Won't you please be seated?" the Commodore insisted. "Take this chair and I'll bring you some of the finest maps you ever saw—blue, green and yellow streams. You needn't explain at all; I know why you are here. You have come from the snow banks to buy orange land, away down below here on the Suwanee. Yes, and I assure you that I would go there myself but the atmosphere down there is a little too lazy for me. That's right; sit down. Yes, I like some little bustle and activity, you know. I ought to be in the north right now. Why, the same energy that I put into this business would soon make me a capitalist in Chicago. But I'm not greedy. Let me see, you would want about forty-five acres. Widow?"

"No, sir."

"Not married, then. Can't always tell, you know. But if you are not married men must be brick-hearted where you came from. Now, I'll get map No. 1 and show you—"

"Pardon me, Mr.—Mr.—Adams, I believe—'

" **Yes**; Commodore Adams."

" Well, Commodore," she said, smiling, " I hope I commit no offence when I tell you that I haven't come to buy land."

The Commodore was startled, and with a puff of astonishment he exclaimed:

" Then, what in the name of heaven could have brought you into this den—into this commercial atmosphere?"

" Why, I saw your advertisement, and I have come to apply for the place."

" Saw the advertisement!" shouted the Commodore. " Why that's remarkable. How did it happen?"

" I bought some oranges on a boat and the paper was wrapped about them."

" Singular, I assure you," said the Commodore. " Peculiar way to put up oranges, but such is fate. So you want the place? That's strange, too. But I don't see why a woman shouldn't assist me. Women have great patience —they know how to wait. Would you be so kind—so adventurous, if you desire to put it that way—as to tell me your name?"

" My name is Rose Sibley."

" Yes, so I hear," said the Commodore, musing. " Rose Sibley. Now I'll have to be frank with you—

it isn't very business-like. And business is what I want, you know." He settled into a deeper musing and the woman sat there smiling. " Rose Sibley," he repeated. " Now, the Sibley part is all right, but I don't know about Rose. However, we could change it if we should find that it interfered with business."

There was a sudden ring of music—she had sprurg from her chair and was laughing at him.

" That's good," he said; " very fine; do it again."

She sobered instantly and resumed her seat; and he looked at her, not with his pretense of fierceness, but with admiration, and when he spoke again it was with more of dignity and earnestness.

" I will not presume to say that you can not acceptably fill the place," he said. " I wouldn't risk an opinion that you could not fill any place." He reflected for a few moments and the atoms which composed his dignity must have shifted, for he looked hard at her and said: " I'll tell you something if you won't say anything about it—my business isn't the success I could wish it. It wrings me to make this confession, but it's a fact. Perhaps I should not have imparted this delicate secret, but there's something about you that in-

spires frankness. But I am not a pauper.
People may tell you that I earned my title and
made some little money by desperately running blockades during the war, but let us not
dwell upon that. But you continue to inspire frankness and I must therefore tell you more
about myself. Slanderers say that what I
possess I made in the cypress swamps, getting
out shingles, but even that would be no disgrace.
I am a gentleman and I can prove it; I am an educated man and I would swear to it. And now,
taking into consideration the fact that Rose is not
business-like, and at the same time admitting that
Sibley is, how can we get at a just remuneration
for your services? I have run up against a good
many commercial problems in my time, but this
is a sticker. Rose on one hand, Sibley on the
other. Ah, where are you from?"

" The west."

" Ah, hah, we'll put that on the Sibley side of
the balance. Now, what have you been doing?"

" I was an art student in—"

" What! Well, that must go on the Rose side."

" In Chicago," she added.

" Oh, well, then, we'll put it on the Sibley side.
Now, let me see. Can't you come around some
time next week? Any time next week will do."

" No. If you think that I can fill the position you must engage me now. I have no time to waste."

" Then why should you want to go into this business ? Let me see. Salary is the only question, miss. I can't afford to pay a great deal, although to engage you would greatly enlarge my scope. I've got a lot of land below here, and with some one in the office I might get out and with my great energy open up a market. You didn't get much of a salary as an art student, I reckon."

She laughed. " No, none at all."

" Ah, hah, and even a small salary here would be better than that. Suppose we start off with twenty dollars a month. How about that figure ? "

" I accept it."

" When can you go to work ? "

She reached up, took a long black pin out of her hair, removed her hat, and said: " I am ready."

" Good. Give me your hat and I'll hang it up. Thank you. There are pens and ink. There's a map. Land is down the river. Write a circular; we'll have it printed and send it over the country. Well," he added when he had hung up her hat, " I bid you good morning."

She looked out after him as he turned down the shaded street, and then spread out a map and began to study it, but soon putting it aside, she placed her arms upon the desk and sat there, musing, with her eyes half closed.   To any one who might have chanced to look into the room, a few moments before the " business man " withdrew, it would have been a matter of but small wonder that the Commodore had forgotten to look upon her with his pretense of fierceness, that he had regarded her with admiration.   She was not tall, but her figure was impressive, with an unexpected dignity.   Her hair was black, her eyes were blue and soft, and her face was rather pale. In the harmony of her features, there was a strange sort of beauty, a beauty that bespoke a mystery.   She had attracted much attention as she walked along the street; her movements seemed to be constantly changing, as if she unconsciously sought to keep pace with her impulses, now slow, and then suddenly breaking into quick and long strides as if keeping step with a long legged man.   From the railway station she had come on a horse, and the horse had been ridden back by a negro boy.   And already the question was passed from one to another: " Who is she ? " The mayor and the town marshal, the four alder·

men and the justice of the peace had seen her—
wise men studying the good of the community—
and had called for an expression of opinion concerning her. The negro boy had been over-
hauled, but the only information he could give was
that she had got off the train and that he had
been sent with her to bring the horse back. And
now as she sat in the Commodore's office, the
mayor and the town council slowly paraded past
the open door and looked in upon her. But she
saw them not, for she was dreaming.

CHAPTER II.

During several hours the Commodore let the wise men indulge in their speculations, and then he told them that he had sent for her. " Gentlemen," said he, standing in front of the tavern, " I have decided to wake this town up. We are somewhat out of the winter-resort circle, though I am sure we have the best on the face of the earth, and I thought it necessary for me to do something to whoop up the lazy echoes of this place; so I sent out west and at an enormous salary secured the services of what is known as a ' land-boomer.' And, sir, that young woman, as beautiful as she appears, is as wise as a saw."

" As a what ? " the mayor asked.

" As a saw, I said. Shakespeare speaks of wise saws, you doubtless remember. I know I do—I mastered him while I was at sea; issued an order to serve him with grog to the men, and when the war was over I had the most dramatic set of seamen on the face of the briny. Yes, gentlemen; I am going to whoop up my land down the river and will also create a demand for real estate in this town. Yes, gentlemen, you who have given the Commodore credit for his honor and his gallantry, will now be compelled to add one other quality—push."

The tavern bells had rung, and looking up the street, the mayor and the aldermen saw the young woman coming to dinner. The Commodore stepped forward as she drew near, and with a salute called out, " Gentlemen, I wish to present you to Miss Rose Sibley, my assistant. Miss Sibley, this is our mayor, General Curtis; this is our marshal, Colonel Black; and these gentlemen are our councilmen, Majors Gray, Perkins, Harper and Brown—all good American names, let me assure you."

She bowed to each one, said that she was pleased to meet so distinguished a company, smiled at the mayor, and gracefully passed into the tavern.

" A beautiful and accomplished lady," said the mayor; " but I fear that as she comes simply with a business recommendation, our society will hesitate a long time before receiving her."

The Commodore touched the brass anchor that he wore on his cap. " I don't think that she has need to fear the restrictions which society draws about itself," he replied. " In truth, in the general rush which may now at any time come upon this town, society may forget to put up some of its draw-bars. But my assistant, sir, will ask no favors."

" Surely not," rejoined the mayor, coughing huskily. " I was merely citing what she might expect. We will wait a while and then I will invite her to my house; but you must know that a lone woman is always under suspicion, and the handsomer she is, the greater the mistrust. But we'll let that drop. You remember three years' ago when Avery came here looking for a pulpit; well, I was the only man that gave him any encouragement. People said that he was a tramp preacher and that no good could be expected of him. I reminded them, you understand, that pretty much the same thing had been held of the Saviour; and finally they let him preach and he stirred up their cold hearts with a fire-brand. Still they were suspicious, but they weakened somewhat when the preacher leaped into the river to rescue a boy from drowning. It wasn't time, however, for a complete surrender. Super-conscious respectability is a mighty hard fighter. They wanted to know why he had wandered off from his folks. Who were his folks, any way ? A man without folks couldn't amount to anything. And they were whetting their knives to split still smaller hairs when the preacher knocked a fellow down for insulting a lady in the street. Then they said that he could preach sure enough; then they agreed that he must have folks; and then he sent to New Haven, Conn., and brought his mother and his sister. But I beg your pardon for this long harangue. Hello, what's the matter up the street?"

There had arisen a loud clamor of voices; men were seen scattering and uniting again in wavering groups, again to be broken and again to unite. Now it was the town marshal's time to make himself felt, and gripping his hickory plant, he ran up the street, the Commodore, the mayor and the board of aldermen following him. In a corner formed by the wall of a building and a high fence, stood a man with a long knife in his hand; and on the opposite side of the street lay a man with his throat cut. The man in the corner was known as Jim, the Swamp Angel. At one time a reward had been offered for him, but his desperate fearlessness had awed cupidity into a tremulous scare, and so the law conveniently forgot that a price had been set upon him. After a long time he came forward, stood his trial, proved that he had a right to shoot a fellow named Hickerson, and went clear.   Now he had assumed the right to cut a man's throat, and a crowd gazed at him as he stood there gripping his knife.   That the brave are always gentle is a fallacy.   This fellow knew not fear and he was a ruffian.

When the town marshal came up and caught the significance of the duty that confronted him, he waved his hickory plant and called upon the fellow to drop his knife. Jim, the Swamp Angel, laughed at him.

" Go on home, Chuffy, and tend your onions," he said.

" Shoot him down!" cried the marshal.

" No," replied the mayor; " that would be no credit.   He must be taken alive.   Where's the Commodore ? "

" Here, your honor, but to tell you the truth i had a chill last night."

The Swamp Angel snorted. " You might as well surrender," said the Mayor, " for if we can't take you one way we will another."

" All right; you'll have to take me the other."

" You see that it is impossible for you to get away."

" That's what you said once before."

" Yes, and the reason you got away that time

was because no gentleman wanted to stain his
hands with your blood."

"Yeah, and no gentleman wanted me to stain
my hands with hizn.'"

"You can't climb that fence and you can't
come this way, so there you are."

"No, here I am."

"Gentlemen," said the mayor, "we'll have to
kill him. I will ask you one more time. Will
you drop that knife and hold up your hands?"

"Come around next week. Ain't in at present."

"Give me your pistol," said the mayor, speaking to the marshal. And just at that moment
there was another stir in the crowd. A tall man,
pale and with his head erect, with his eyes turned
upward, was slowly parting a way toward the
mayor; and when he reached him, he lowered
his glance, and in his eyes there shone a light,
strong and clear. He placed his hand on the pistol which the mayor was raising, and he said,
"No, don't shoot him."

"Mr. Avery, I have great respect for you, sir,
but I must shoot him. He has poured blood on
the law. Look over there." He pointed to
the dead man.

Avery did not look. "You must not shoot

him," he repeated. "Wait." He took the pistol from the mayor's hand, dropped it on the ground, and then slowly but boldly walked toward the Swamp Angel. A cry arose and the mayor shouted at him, but onward he went, with his strong, clear gaze fixed upon the man in the corner.

"If you come in reach I'll kill you!" cried the Swamp Angel. But the man continued slowly to advance, and a silence lay upon the crowd.

"Stop!" cried the Swamp Angel, and he raised his knife. The man took two more steps, raised his hand, took the knife, grasped the Swamp Angel by the arm, led him to the street—and the crowd shouted.

"Marshal," said the conqueror, "take him to jail. Gentlemen, stand about that dead body. Here comes a lady."

The officers led the Swamp Angel away, and the crowd stood about the body. Avery, the preacher, the master of the Swamp Angel, took off his hat, bowed to Rose Sibley, and said: "Don't look over there, please. Come this way. Thank you."

She said nothing but she gazed at him, and he touched his eyes with his hand, and as he put on his hat, when she had passed on, his hand trembled.

When the jailer had turned the key upon the Swamp Angel, he looked at the subdued man and .asked:

" Were you afraid of him?"

" No, damn him, his look fazed me and I forgot my knife."

CHAPTER III.

The law took solemn charge of the body that lay in the street, the marshal bravely waving off the boys that had gathered there to look in awe upon it. The Commodore and the preacher slowly strolled toward the real estate office.

" You've got the trick that old Andy Jackson had," said the Commodore. " They say he could look at a man and make him give up; and once I recollect seeing a man do the very same thing you did just now. But I can't do it. How did you manage it ?"

" I did not manage it at all," the preacher answered. " I didn't think. If I had thought, perhaps I might have been frightened, and then he would have killed me. That young woman went to your office, I believe?"

" Yes, haven't you heard about her? I reckon she is one of the most remarkable women in this country, sir. I've had my mind's eye on her for a long time; have noticed her brilliant achievements in real estate. So I resolved to bring her here, and after a long correspondence she decided to come, but it was hard work to get her here. I assure you.   Won't you come in ?"

They were now standing at the door.   Avery hesitated. " I believe I will," he said, and stepped into the room.   The young woman was standing in front of a map hanging on the wall.   The Commodore took off his cap and with a sweeping flourish introduced the preacher.   She smiled at him, bowed, and turned again to the map.

" Miss Sibley," said the Commodore, " I've seen a good many preachers in my time, but Avery here is the gamest one I ever saw.   It isn't every community that can boast of a game preacher, I tell you; and this fact alone ought to sell our immediate real estate if we put it in our circular.   It's a fact, miss."

Over her shoulder she was looking at him, laughing at him; and the preacher was smiling at her.

" The Commodore would put me forth as quite a desperate character.   Pardon me," he added, " but from what part of the country do you come ?"

" From the west," she answered, looking full into his eyes, looking as though she would read him; and he put his hand to his eyes and his hand was tremulous.

"From the mountains," she added, still looking at him.

" But your accent is too soft for one from the
west," he said.

She smiled, and again turning to the map replied: " Perhaps I am from the sunny side of a
mountain."

" Avery, that ain't bad," the Commodore joined
in. " Sunny side of a mountain—good fruit land,
apples and peaches; yes, sir, the sunny side of a
mountain is all right. We've got some hill land
on our list. But put it into the circular as the
sunny side of a mountain. Avery, she's getting
up a circular and we are going to scatter copies
of it broad-cast over the country. I'd have my
own daughter write it, but she's too literary; puts
in too many flowers—make her fortune some day
in the book business. That's what they used to
say when she was a child, away up yonder in
East Tennessee, and I'm getting to believe it.
Well, reckon I'll walk over to the jail to see if
they've got that fellow in there all right. Won't
do to have him running loose on the community."

Avery sat down—when the Commodore withdrew. Miss Sibley continued to study the map.

" I suppose," said the preacher, " that it took
you several years to master the details of this in-
tricate business ?"

" I don't know how long it may take me," she replied. " I am now at the beginning. My experience began this morning."

" What ! Why, the Commodore says that you are a wonderful expert."

" Does he ? Then I must not dispute his word. Yes, I am a great expert."

" Ah, but then how can it be that your experience has just begun ? "

" Oh, we must leave that to the Commodore," she answered, leaving off her study of the map and taking a seat at the desk. She drew a pad of paper toward her and began to write rapidly with a pencil, and he looked at her, studied her. And when she looked up he started.

" I take an interest in you because you are a stranger," he said.

" And not because I am a woman ? " she asked.

He pretended to laugh, but her quick eye saw that he was not mirthful; he was red and embarrassed.

" I didn't know that you would turn it that way," he said, looking thoughtfully at her." Perhaps I would better have said, ' a stranger and a woman.' I came hither three years ago and was looked upon with suspicion, and I know what it is to feel strange. The Southerner is suspicious until he knows one; he is a sentinel at the out-posts of society, waiting for the countersign, and you cannot pass in until it has been given, but once within the lines, you find there a cheering welcome; and standing about, thoughtfully waiting, are warm and generous friendships. I have preached in several places.   After leaving New Haven, wherein I was born and reared, I went forth in search of a pulpit.   I was not disposed to accept a narrow set of rules; I looked for independence.   I wanted to preach the divine doctrine of love.   That was all the creed that I could gather unto myself.   In my heart I felt a love that sprang and flamed into life, one night while I was on my knees, praying for wisdom. I could gather knowledge, but wisdom was beyond my reach.   Yes, a love leaped into my heart, and then there was no room for creed.   It is not a love for mankind, nor for truth nor virtue —it is a love for the man who trod the hot sands of Galilee, a passionate love, a love that came to rule me.   And instead of making me a bigot, it has made me liberal.   I can scarcely bring myself to blame a man who does evil.   I feel that it is not his fault, for the love that I feel has been withheld **from him.   No determination of his could draw** down that love, and if it has been denied him, it is surely not his fault."

She had put back her writing pad; her arms were resting on the desk, and she was looking at him.

" But wouldn't you blame one for committing murder ? " she asked.

" I would pity more than blame," he answered.

" Yes, but wouldn't you have the murderer punished ? "

" Surely. Oh, I don't pardon crime, don't justify sin, and yet I feel that it is not wholly the fault of the criminal. And this doctrine, if we may call it such, together with a few liberal ideas concerning the conduct of man, drove me out of three pulpits. At last I came to this place. I preached and the people appeared to like me, but I know that they would not have tolerated my views had I not shown myself to be a man, more of a man than a preacher. The Southerner is an admirer of a fearless man. He thinks that bravery is honor; and here it is better for a preacher to be a hero among men than a saint among women."

" And you proved yourself a hero to-day," she said.

"No, I did my duty. It wasn't bravery. I looked at that fellow and I felt that he would not harm me. It was a confidence inspired by the passionate love that came to me at night. You must really pardon me," he suddenly spoke up, arising. "I am robbing you of your time."

"Oh, no, I can do this work to-night."

"But it would be a cruelty to impose it upon you when you should be asleep. I hope that I have not bored you."

"You have interested me. But as a general thing preachers don't please me. They may seek to console a man, but they strive to flatter a woman. They seem to think that a certain meek polish is all that is required to make them acceptable to society; they give us a flat homily and would have us accept it for a rounded truth."

He stood looking down into her eyes, and after a time, still looking at her, he said: "You astonish me."

"With what I have said? Would it have astonished you had a man said it?"

"No," he frankly acknowledged. She was silent and he turned to go, but at the door he halted and faced about.

"You are staying at the hotel, I believe?"

" Yes; for the present."

" Would you grant my mother and sister the privilege of calling upon you this evening ? "

" It would be a kindness rather than a privilege."

He bowed and said, " I thank you."

She sat there and mused a long time after he had gone, and she remembered that he was graceful, handsome; remembered this, but his eyes haunted her. She strove to picture him as he had sat there, as he had stood there, but she saw only his eyes, strong, glowing; she bent her ear as if to catch the echo of his voice, but she heard it not. His eyes were haunting her.

CHAPTER IV.

The mother and the sister had called and Miss Sibley had been induced to board at their home. And how romantic a place it was. An old brick house on a swell of ground, overlooking the river. From her window she could see far down the stream; could look into a mellow twilight that like the gray moss seemed to hang from the trees. The garden sloped down to the water's edge, and the vines crept close to the rippling tide; and the shrubbery leaned over and caught roses that drifted from far above. At morning, bright birds came thither to drink, and when the cool of the evening was come, back again they flew to twitter and to sing. The house was the oldest in the community, had been built, it was said, by a Spaniard. The negroes declared it haunted, and during a number of years it had stood vacant.

The smaller trees were ragged and needed trimming, the garden was wild, but Avery said that nothing must be changed, no briars cut down, no

boughs lopped off.   The garden was his wilderness, and into it he went to shape his sermons.

The mother was a stout old lady.   She always
wore a cap, said " I want to know! " and was
proud of her son, not particularly of his manliness, his courage, but of the grace which the
Lord had given unto him.   The girl was younger
than Miss Sibley.   Her name was Ellen, and for
it she expressed a great contempt.   She was an
enemy of all practical things.   She said that in
this life there should be nothing save romance.
A business man could not be a lover; arithmetic
was the enemy of poetry, and poetry was love.

She was a lithe and handsome girl, bright and
pettish; and languishing suitors had come to her
—a rich orange grower, a western cattle man, a
neighboring merchant, a poor but dignified South-
ern gentleman—but one by one she had sent them
away.   She was dreaming of the poet yet to come,
and she pleaded for the solitude of the tangled
garden.   The mother, thrifty and sensible Yankee,
placed no approval upon this foolishness.   To
see her daughter well settled was a natural desire,
a laudable yearning.   She had but short patience
with the visionary poet to come, the fog-form
roseate in the east; the cattle man suited her.
She said that a well-appointed home was the

truest and most lasting poem, and observation had shown her that the commonplace man was the best husband.

"You have lost the chance of your life," she said to her daughter when the cattleman had departed; "you have thrown away a fortune."

"But I haven't sold myself, mother," the girl replied. "I didn't love him; I couldn't sell my love."

"Love—fiddlesticks. Get a home and the love will come. Not sold your love? Well, I want to know! Liza Pruett didn't sell her love, either. Oh, no; she married it. And what about her now? Three ragged children and a drunken poet."

"But mother, all poets are not drunkards."

"Mighty few of them that ain't, I tell you. Lucy Simons just *had* to marry a man that wrote stories. Oh, he was so romantic and could talk so sweetly! And now what? She's back at home and he's poked off somewhere. And look at Josh Aimes, that wanted to marry her. What about him? Got rich in the soap business. If ever a man comes on this place and I think he's a poet I will scald him. He shan't drag a daughter of mine down to want."

"But, mother, there is no hurry. I'm young enough to wait."

" Ah, but opportunities are not; **they don't** wait. I warrant you that Rose Sibley would have taken that cattle man. Just look at her, compelled to earn her own living, and she's a sight smarter than you'll ever be. That fool blowing about how much he pays her! She makes a bare living and that's all. And I wish I knew more about her. I can't make her out, I'm sure. Says she's from the West and that's all there is to it. Ah, hah, and when your poet comes you may find that he was once her husband."

" Mother, for gracious sake don't talk that way! I wouldn't have that get out for anything. She is one of the family, and you must be more careful. I'm sure I have never seen a nobler girl than she is. She understands me, and that's more than I can say for most people. Why is it, mother, that you don't talk money to brother Louis?"

" Your brother is quite different. He has a mission. And here he comes now through the garden with Miss Sibley."

It was evening, and Rose was coming from work. The preacher had met her at the garden gate. Slowly they strolled along a briar-bound path, and Avery was deftly parting the thorns to let her pass. They reached a cleared place,

whereon had stood a summer house, and on the
mouldering ruin they halted, looking down the
river.   The air grew sweeter as night came on;
twilight drew a perfume too timid, too delicate
to trust itself abroad in the glow of the sun.
Humming low a night fly came, side by side with
a negro melody; a church bell sounded, and the
rippling stream drew down the sad tone, bore it
away and buried it in a lily bed.

The preacher was looking at the woman, and
his eyes were soft; down the river she was gazing,
and her eyes were spiritual.

" The sweetness in the air is the breath of
God," he said.

And still gazing far away, she replied, " The
sweetness in the air is nature, forgetfully mus'
ing."

" But God is nature."

" Perhaps," she assented.

" But why should there be a perhaps; can
there be a doubt?   Nature creates—God is a cre-
ator."

" It is not for a woman to argue with a
preacher," she said, looking at him; and he saw
and felt her eyes, though the darkness was deep-
ening.

" Why do you continuously refer to me as a

preacher ?   You seem to have a contempt for the word."

" You constantly remind me that you are a preacher.   But I think that a man is nobler than a priest; and you are a man.   So why not let me forget that you are a priest ?"

" It would be strange that I could inspire you with any sort of forgetfulness when you inspire me with so many thoughts.   I wish that I might ask you to be perfectly frank with me." *

Her laugh was as low and as musical as the rippling of the river.   " I can't be perfectly frank with you," she said.   " I can't be perfectly frank with myself.   I was once rather frank with a man—"

" What about him ?" he quickly asked.

" Oh, there's nothing about him."

He cleared his throat with a rasp of disappointment, of annoyance.

" If you did not intend to say more you should not have mentioned him."

" Perhaps not.   Shall we go to the house ?"

" Yes, in a moment.   I like to talk to you and I so rarely see you alone.   Where were you educated ?"

' I have seen Wellesly."

" And you are how old ?"

"I am old enough to feel that I am wiser than I was, and yet young enough to believe that I shall know more."

"You may not be frank with me, but I am going to be frank with you. I am interested in you."

"What a desperate confession," she replied, laughing.

"Why are you here? Why did you come?"

He had expected to hear her laugh again, but she did not. She sighed. "It is not my wish to appear mysterious, Mr. Avery," she said, "but I can tell you absolutely nothing with regard to myself. If you urge me I might tell an untruth, and I never do this except as a matter of self defense. I love truth, but I can't always tell it. You say you are interested in me; and now I will be frank: don't let that interest bend your judgment. I like you—like your mother and sister, and I am grateful when I realize that I am one of the family; I don't know how long I may remain here, but I shudder to think of going away, for rest lies along the banks of this river. Shall we walk on?"

"One word more. I am stronger than you, and I know it; I have more force than you—more of that intellectual animalism which commands.

which insists upon obedience—I have this, for my passionate love for the Galilean inspires it —and yet you—you treat me as I treat this." He grasped a fig tree and violently shook it. "But you will find," he added, pulling the slender tree toward him and tightly gripping it— "you will find that the priest is but the weakest part of me. Wait just a moment. Your name is the name of the queen of flowers; were it anything else, I could call you Miss; as it is I must call you Rose; may I ?"

"Yes, for it is a truth that I do not deny."

"I don't understand you."

"Your mother is calling you," she said.

In the parlor the lamp was lighted; at the open window an old vine was murmuring in the breeze that came up the river.

Mrs. Avery met them at the door. "Louis," she said, "your time is short. Don't you know that this is prayer meeting night ? The bell has rung."

"I know it now, mother, but I had forgotten it."

She gave him a sharp glance and replied: "Well, I want to know—a minister forgetting to pray! "

"It is not likely that you will let me **forget**

that I am a minister." He opened the piano.
" Ellen, sing something."

" Supper is ready, brother."

" Rose," he said, " play something." She
was standing near the piano, but she drew back
with a shudder. " No," she said; " you must
not ask me to play—you must never ask me
again."

" Conscience alive!" the old lady exclaimed;
" what on earth is the matter with everybody to-
night ? Ellen has been fretting the life out of
me over her fool poet and—"

" Mother! "

" Yes, you have; and now my son forgets to
pray."

" Madam," said the preacher, " I will not
pray to-night; I will send Jude to tell them that
I will not be there." He stepped to the window
and loudly called " Jude!" and out in the dark a
voice answered, " Comin', sah." An old negro
soon appeared at the door, crumpling his hat in
his hand.

" Jude, go to the church and tell them that I
shall not be there to-night."

" Tell them that my son is not well," Mrs.
Avery spoke up.

" Tell them nothing of the sort, Jude," the

preacher interposed. "But if they ask you if I am well, tell them yes."

"I'll do dat, sah; do dat caze you tells me ter, still I doan think it's de bes' plan. You'se libed yeah er good w'ile, sah, but you wa'n't bawned yeah; an'—an'—'

"Go on, Jude."

"Yas, sah, dat's what I'se doin'—doin' it ez fas' ez I kin', but de Skripter say, 'Come yeah an' lemme reason wid you,' an' dat's what I wanter do, caze I'se er older pusson den you is, an' 'sides dat I wuz bawned yeah. Well, I mus' be gwine, now; an' atter I comes back I'd like ter slip in yeah an' git er few mou'fuls o' yo' grace, sah. I finds dat de older er man gits de mo' grace he need. Gwine now, caze I'se in er monstus hurry."

"Go on, and when you return you may come in here."

"Now I know I'm gone. Wa'n't sho o' it at fust, but I knows it now."

At last he was gone. The preacher sat on the piano stool with his elbows thrust back upon the keys.

"Miss Sibley," said Mrs. Avery, "may I see you alone a moment?"

Rose followed her into the hall, into a corner

where the light from the parlor lamp fell dimmest.

" What is the matter with my son ?" the old lady asked. " Tell me without any beating about, for I am a straightforward woman. Nothing would do him but that you must come here to board, and now, in this short time, he has undergone a complete change. What is the matter with him?"

" If I don't answer you as readily as you may think that honesty demands, Mrs. Avery, you must not put it down as unwillingness but as ignorance. I don't know what is the matter with him; I don't know that anything ails him."

" Miss Sibley, you are beating about. He is my son, and every change in him makes me anxious. I don't wish to question your honesty, but you came here so strangely—"

" And I will go away so naturally."

" Oh no, now, don't say that. You misunderstand me. His word is law with me, and if he wishes you to stay here you must; indeed, I want you to stay. I like you, although I can't find out anything about you and—well, you know, we are all more or less peculiar. But—and you will pardon me now, won't you ?—but you won't persuade him to leave the pulpit. I believe that my prayers placed him there. I may be a crank, but I can't help making this request of you. I

have never seen him influenced by ary one so
much as he is by you, and although I have
always lived a strict and narrow life, yet I must
say that I believe you are a good woman, although you won't tell us all about yourself.
Won't you promise me?"

Rose placed her hands upon the old lady's
cheeks, drew her head forward, looked into her
eyes; and the mother, tremulous between those
slender and graceful hands, waited not for a reply
in words. "I believe you," she said; "I have
confidence in you. It is all so strange, I am
sure!"

"What are you doing out here?" Louis
Avery was standing in the door, looking upon
them. "What does this sly conference mean,
mother?"

"Oh, nothing, I assure you," she answered,
slowly moving toward him. "I had something
that I wanted to say to Rose and—"

"You were talking about me, mother. I wish
you wouldn't. I am not a child. I am almost a
giant in size."

"But a giant is the child of his mother, my
son. Come in, Rose."

There was a fireplace in the room, and it was
filled with the boughs of a spicewood tree, and with

flowers; in front of it Ellen stood, her shapely
head resting against the mantle-piece.

"Oh, I wish had something to read," she said.
"You people do make it awfully lonesome for
me at times; but—I am going to call you Rose, if
brother does—I say, I am sure you could tell me
some romantic adventures of your own. Oh,
you've had them, and don't say you haven't."

Rose had sat upon the piano stool, but she ac-
cidently touched a key, and getting up quickly
she went to the window and sat there, looking
out.

"Won't you, please," Ellen pettishly insisted.

"I have no romances to tell," Rose answered.
"They say that romance is coming back," she
added, laughingly, but without turning from
the window, still looking out into the darkness
that lay upon the tangled garden—"they say
that romance is coming back, and when it reaches
me I may then tell you one."

"I wish you would tell it now. Why, romance
has never been driven away from this place."

"That's true, Ellen," Louis spoke up. "Romance, like the Indian, has been driven about, but
this piace was set aside as a reservation. Oh, I
love the South; not for its new blast furnaces,
nor for any promise of material wealth, but for

a certain shiftlessness, for its wastefulness. I hate
economy, and here nature is not an economist.
Nature is a thoughtless spendthrift; and love is a
spendthrift; the Galilean was a spendthrift, for at
the hearts of all men he threw His jewels—the
rubies and the diamonds of his love. In the eyes
of society, of the law, he was a vagabond, and I
love him for that. He was the truest of all Bohe-
mians, a wandering genius, looking for a place to
rest His head. He was the most homeless of all
tramps; He touched a vice and glorified it into a
virtue. He was not looking for the economical,
the righteous. He frowned upon rules, forms, set
modes of existence. I care nothing about His
birth; I don't reflect upon a holy conception; I
care not for the manner of His coming, or why
He came. All I care to know, to feel, is that I
love Him; and loving Him, I hate churches."

" Louis!" his mother cried, and Rose turned
from the window. " Louis, you will lose another
pulpit if you talk like that. Remember that
three times you have been driven away."

" No, mother, I remember that three times I
have been led away. Would you have me be
dishonest with myself and unfaithful to the divine
Bohemian?"

"There are some thoughts which we must all

keep to ourselves," Rose remarked, looking at him, admiring him. "No one can hold you accountable for what you think—you can't hold yourself accountable for that—but when you say a thing it is no longer solely your own, but belongs in part to other people; and sometimes they resent the ownership thus put upon them. If I were you I would say nothing to weaken the respect of the congregation; I would find out what sort of preaching they want, and—no, I won't say that."

The preacher thanked her for not saying it, but the mother, eager for any opinion that might tend to make her son discreet, urged the young woman to complete the sentence.

But she would not. She said that to have begun it was on her part an impertinence. Why should she presume to offer advice? And above all, why should she seek to explore the ethics of a pastor's duty?

The negro man appeared at the door, and the preacher, who had stiffened himself with a homily, loosened his tension and told the old man to come in. He dropped his hat at the door, but catching an impatient motion made by the preacher, caught it up, laughed, and said: "I kai git outen thinkin' dat it's manners fur me ter drap my hat at de do'. I'se er ole time nigger an' I kai furgait it. Wall, sah, I wen' ter de church, an' I tole de folks dat I 'gretted it mightily but dat de Sheapard couldn' be dar. One de men 'lowed he knowed you wa'n't well an' I jest let it go at dat; an' I'se monsters sho' dar ain' gwine be no hard feelin's.''

"Sit down, Jude," said the preacher. "Sit down and tell Miss Sibley of your experience in the North."

The old fellow carefully eased himself down upon a chair, dropped his hat on the floor, reached over and took it up with a grunt, turned it round and round and then said:

"W'y dat wa'n't much o'er 'sperience, Miss. Er lot o' cullud men went fum erbout yeah to work on what da called er pipe line, er way up yander, an' I went wid 'em; an' atter de wuck was done, I went wid a nigger generman up ter St. Paul. An' da treated me mighty well up dar, da did, an' I cut a monstus wide swath till de win'er time come, an' den I gins to shiver. De col' win' sung er sad song in de night, an' de shreakin' o' de snow in de street soun' like somebody tryin' to play on er fife. An' dar waz de 'Sippy riber all froze—an' I stood dar an' listened ter it, er gogglin' its froat un'er de

ice. Still I 'lowed I was er doin' putty well, er
workin' roun' er big tavern dar, an' er pickin' up
er quarter ever' now an' den. One night er
porter axed me ter go ter er show wid 'im an'
I went. We tromped er way up stars an' sot
down in de lof', an' bimeby de music 'gins
ter play an' it wuz mighty sweet. But all at once
suthin' wa'm is fillin' me up an' de tears is er
gushin' outen my eyes—er lady was er standin'
on de flatfaum er singin' 'Way down upon
de Suwanee riber!' An' den I jumped up an'
says, 'Lemme git outen yeah—lemme git out, caze
I kai stan' it er minit longer!' Laws er massy,
de wa'm suthin' dat poured ober me! I seed de
ole riber er slippin' er long in de moonlight,
I yeahed it licken' de bank—I seed de trees an'
de moss hangin' down; an' scufflin' dar in dat big
house way up on de frozen 'Sippy, I cried louder
den eber, 'Lemme git outen yeah!' Oh, it made
er big 'sturbance, an' er constable he grabbed me
an' he 'lows dat he gwine put me out. 'Dat's
jest whut I wan' you ter do,' says I, ' an' I want
you ter do it ez quick ez you kin.' Out I went,
an' I goes ter de tavern an' I gedered up my
traps an' got on a kyah an' I come back yere.
Yas, Miss, an' I run right down ter de riber—
right down by dis gyarden—an' stuck my arms in

it an' hugged it. An' I'm gwine stay yeah, too. I kin meck mo' money up yander, but my heart's down yeah on dis riber—by de graves down yander at de bend—an' I'm gwine stay yeah ez long ez de Lawd 'll let me.

CHAPTER V.

The old song was sung. The preacher stood looking at Rose, and his mother sat looking at him. The moon came up above the trees, far down the river, and the girl at the window saw black shadows creeping in the garden. Bed time came, and she sat at her window upstairs, dreaming in the soft air, dreaming over her present anchorage and the causes that had set her adrift. The old woman's anxiety pictured itself, somewhere in the dark, and she stared at it. Again she heard the preacher's avowal of his faith, and she listened half astonished, as she would have listened had a set of church bells turned from their wonted chime to ring a sweet but forbidden tune. She was in that mood which knows the death of old sentiments or the birth of new ones, between tears and a prayer, remembering a sorrow and yet startled by a joy. Into this quiet place, this sentimental sanctuary of an almost endless spring-time, how kindly had she been received. The village people were simple and were curious to know her past, her family, and the reasons why she had left her home, but they were easily put off with a pleasantly worded evasion. Under the patronage of the preacher's family she was respected, and drawn by her own charm of manner, her smile, the soft tones of her voice, her eyes, came admiration. It was said that no one had so easily set aside the prejudices put about a stranger, but she knew that this was not due alone to her herself, but to the bravery, the manliness of her patron.

The moon was now high and the Suwanee was a trail of dimpling light. Far below an island rose like the prow of a great ship, coming up the stream. On the other side, just opposite the garden, the trees, struck aslant by the moon, threw a black edge into the water. She heard the dipping of oars, and out of the black edge shot a boat. Across the stream of light it sped and touched the garden. A man leaped out and pulled the bow of the boat upon the shore. This was nothing, some fisherman, perhaps; but the next moment she saw a form in white gliding down the path toward the river. Was it Ellen? She had that evening been dressed in white. But every woman in the village dressed thus airily. It was Ellen. The man came to meet her, took her into his arms. He led her to the place where the ruins of the summer house were mouldering, and there they stood with their arms about each other. With a sigh Rose turned from the window and sat down to think, not of herself, not of the preacher but of his sister. She felt that some wily stranger had come from the knowing world to steal the affections of this silly child, and one moment she was resolved to save her, but the next instant she drew back from the thought of meddling with the love of two honest and romantic hearts. Perhaps after all the girl was not Ellen. But at morning this self-imposed doubt was cleared away. At breakfast Ellen was dreamy, and in her hair was a wilted flower.

" Ellen," said her mother, looking sharply at the flower, " you don't look as if you've slept a wink. I declare you get worse all the time instead of better. Have you been to bed at all?"

" Why, mother, what questions you can ask. What makes you think I would sit up all night?"

" The poet must have kept her awake," Avery suggested; " though I don't know why," he added. " The majority of rhymers put us to sleep."

" Now, brother, I don't want any sarcasm from you. I want everybody to let me alone, that's what I want. Rose, you understand me Won't you be my friend?"

"Yes, and I may be a friend to your poet if you will only let me see him," Rose answered, looking straight into her eyes, striving to read her.

"Will you? Then when he comes you shall be the first of all my friends to shake hands with him."

"Are you sure that he hasn't already come?"

"Oh, how could he come without my seeing him? Why does everybody look at me as if I hadn't any sense? Louis, don't stare at me that way please. You really make me feel like an idiot. Rose, I'm going to walk as far as the office with you this morning."

The way to the office was called a street, but with the exception of the hotel and a few storehouses that obtruded upon it, the town's Broadway was a lane, hedged with live oaks, festooned with vines. Here and there was an old house, standing far back, gray in the shadow of the hanging moss, touched with that over-maturity which men may call ruin, but which is Old Time's soft and mellowing art.

"What were you going to tell me?" Rose asked as she and Ellen walked along. "What about the poet?"

" I didn't say I was going to tell you anything
—said that I was going as far as the office with
you.   But I could tell you something that would
—would make you think."

" Yes, but did you think?   Do you think of
consequences?"

" Why, of course I do.   What a goose you
must think I am.   But I won't tell you now.
Wait till to-night, for it might not sound so well
while the sun's shining; it's a lamp-light story."

" Isn't it a moon-light story?" Rose asked.

" Why, yes, you could call it that.   Oh, isn't
it charming to be silly?   When I look at a wise
person I always say, 'Oh how unhappy you must
be.'   And you are unhappy, Rose.   Yes, you are;
I know it.   Tell me why."

" It is not because I am wise."

" Yes, it is, for if you were not wise you wouldn't
keep on thinking about it.   Wise people have
to think, or at least they imagine they do.
Well, I'll turn back here.   Yonder's the Commodore, and he always bores me.   I wonder that he
doesn't get tired of himself.   And his daughter
is with him.   Whenever I meet her I'm worn out
for a week afterward.   Good bye.   I'll tell you
to-night."

When Rose entered the office she found the

Commodore and his daughter walking up and down the floor. The affection that existed here was well regulated, and care was taken that it should be well presented. The Commodore loved his daughter because she was the offspring of so distinguished a man, and the daughter appeared to love him for no other reason than that it was the duty of a rising writer to give affection to the obvious cause of her existence. Of course there may have been a real attachment, natural that there should be, but the most credulous and simple minded of us look skeptically upon a paraded regard. The Commodore had heard with an ear that catches vague rumor, that away back somewhere there had lived a be-gowned genius named Sappho, and to the female Adams he had given the name borne to the cliff by the seething-blooded Grecian. He had not investigated the moral character of Sappho the first; he knew not whether she wrote hymns to a mythical God or wound her glowing arms about the bull-neck of a real acrobat. He had heard that she had written, and that was enough. Latterly some one had told him that a French writer created a Sappho, and that she was not morally fitted to sing with the blacksmith's daughters in the village choir, but the Commodore replied that no Frenchman could legislate for him, that he knew his business; and no one in the community wherein he lived at that time was wise enough successfully to dispute with him.

The circulars written by Rose had passed in review under Sappho's searching eye, and they had more often been approved by languor than by judgment; for when her faculties were active, an etching by De Quincey—the Flight of a Tartar Tribe itself—could not have escaped without bleeding. Sappho was tall, thin, hysterical. Her little eyes looked like two peas, shelled too late, a whitish green; and her hair which was thin, gave her great annoyance—it did not look frowsy enough. She was afraid to marry; it was the lot of a literary woman to have trouble in her family. She had often been in love; it was the duty of a fanciful and creative mind to study emotion. A profane but virtuous Irish woman once called her a damned fool, and the Commodore set out to look for her husband, to feast a father's just vengeance upon Celtic blood. But learning that the woman was not married, he swore that he would wait with dignified patience until she secured a husband and that then he would kill the scoundrel.

" Come in, Miss Rose," said the Commodore

"Beautiful day. Shake hands with Sappho. All days are beautiful that hang over our land, eh? That fellow that haggled around yesterday came to my house after supper and closed the deal. That's business; if you can't catch them in the day time grab them at night."

"Oh, father!" exclaimed Sappho, stepping back from him and turning up her eyes.

"Pardon me, my daughter. I did not intend to speak of business in your presence."

"It was such a shock, father."

"Yes, my sweet one, but it was thoughtless on my part. Won't you forgive a hurried and tumbling commercial man?"

"Yes, father," she replied, holding out her hand, and with a bow he kissed it.

"Ah, Miss Rose," said he, "you can now perceive what real gallantry is. Before her hallowed mother was laid away where the jessamines grow, the world had an example of truest consideration and affection, but now in this turmoil of trade—"

"Oh, father, don't."

"Pardon me, my daughter, pardon me. I forgot myself again. And now, precious one, go on and run in sweet riot among the butterflies of your fancy, for Miss Rose and I have our hard

and exacting duties to perform.   When I was. in
the navy, it was my duty to fight; and now in
this turmoil of real estate—but I will say no more.
Run along.   Miss Rose and I are busy."

She bowed, smiled, withdrew; and the Commodore, tilting his chair against the wall, soor.
began to nod.   Rose sat at her desk, musing.
There were no letters to receive attention, no
deeds to be filled out.   There were the maps,
but she had studied them until the red lines were
held by her inner sight like a blood-shot dream.

The Commodore awoke with a snort.   Rose
could see him without turning in her chair, and
she saw that he was looking at her.

" I hope you are not rushing yourself," he said,
rubbing his eyes.   " That business transaction last
night somewhat exhausted me and I feel the need
of sleep.   Let's see, I'm paying you twenty dollars.   And now, in view of the recent spurt affairs have taken, I'll make it twenty-five."

" I am exceedingly obliged to you, Commodore."

" Miss, dear Miss, I pray you to feel no obli-
gation.   I am a rough sailor, used to desperate
strife upon the deep, but I hope that I know how
to treat a lady.   And if you should ever **need a
friend**—"

"I thank you, Commodore."

"No, thank yourself, your own nature. I say that if you ever need a friend turn with confidence to the old salt."

He felt for his cap to touch the brass anchor, but he was bare-headed. "Let the motion serve for the deed," he said. "I will always be your friend. Tell me, how are you and the preacher getting along?"

She was not looking at him now. She was "bunching" the circulars that lay on the desk.

"Oh, we get along very well."

"I thought you would; but he is really a peculiar man. He is brave—wish he had been with my fleet—brave, and the people love him for that, but sometimes they don't like the way he preaches. Our people, you know, are very religious, and Brother Avery doesn't denounce sin quite strong enough. Here sometime ago a gambler came up the river, came to skin the citizens, understand. Well, Sunday came, and as there was no other place to go he went to church to pick out a few victims. And what does Brother Avery do? He stepped down out of the pulpit when the fellow entered the church, walked forward, took him by the hand and led him to a front seat. That might be all right in some places, but here it won't do."

" Did the gambler skin any of the citizens, as you term it ?"

" Well, no. He went down the river the next morning."

" And don't you suppose that the preacher's act was better than an interference on the part of the law?"

" It was all well enough, but it didn't look exactly right in church, and on Sunday, too. And now Brother Avery persists in saying something to keep the resentment alive. Ain't content with giving out the gospel as the Book has shown it to him—has to twist it a little."

" They'll never get another man like him," Rose said, sitting back in her chair, looking not at the Commodore, but upward. " He is true, and true men are not to be found every day, even though we search the priesthood."

" By George, Miss, it's just such remarks as these that knock me down every time I begin to think that I am standing up pretty well in front of you. We might naturally expect such talk from a man that had just been bit in a land trade, but I'll be hanged if we expect it from a woman who ought to be putting in her odd time in thanking God for her brightness and her beauty. Pardon me, I am but a rough seaman, an outlawed sailor, but I have picked up some of the wisdom that has fallen to the land-lubber, and am, there fore—I might say—therefore not a fool. Of course woman is now supposed to have almost as much sense as man—I say supposed—and she is assuming the right to express her thoughts, but she ought never to be cynical. We don't expect to find dry dust in a ripe peach. Now, here, that's not bad," he added, scratching his head. "Dry dust in a peach—I'll tell it to Sappho. Come in, Jude." The old negro was standing at the door. "Come in and state your business as quickly as you can. We are in a great rush to-day."

"Yas, sah," Jude replied, dropping his hat. "I war er passin,' sah, an' I didn' know but de young Miss, heah, mout want a bucket o' fraish water about dis time o' day."

"All right, there's the bucket. And stir your stumps, Jude, for we're in a great rush to-day."

"Yas, sah, I 'lowed you wuz w'en I seed you er settin' yeah. Yas, sah, yas, sah," he hastened to add to cover up his gentle sarcasm; "I knows you'se stirrin' things up. Met Mr. Avery down yander, talkin' ter some folks on de cawndah o' de street, an' he mus' er been er talkin' grace, fur de mayor wuz a settin' on er box, noddin'. Er huh, huh. 'Pear like folks keeps outen de grace laung ez da kin. Yas, sah, I'se gwine now."

The Commodore arose and walked up and down the room. It was not alone an unwonted rush of business that seemed to be disturbing his mind; another cause had moved him to restlessness. He went to the door and looked up and down the street; he called to Jude to hasten with the water, but when the water was brought, he drank not. He took the bucket, placed it upon a shelf built against the wall, and dismissed the negro. He took up his chair, placed it near Rose's desk, sat down, tried to look fierce, whistled softly and then was silent, staring at the opposite wall.

" And the wisdom that I have caught," he said, jerking himself out of his abstraction—" the wisdom that was thrown by a wasteful Providence to the land-lubbers, teaches me that loneliness makes a woman cynical. Ah," he suddenly exclaimed, slapping himself, " ah but why should a woman be lonely? There is a fine point, Miss Rose. Why should a woman be lonely? What makes her lonely? The absence of love. Miss Rose, I know that you have not been looking around for love, for the most precious boon, I may say, of that sort comes upon us out of an ambush. My heart is an ambush, Miss Rose, and my love, I might say, has sprung out at you. There now, please don't get up. Rush of business, you know. Wait, won't you, please?"

Rose was now standing at the window, looking out. " I won't take up but a few moments of your valuable time," the Commodore went on. " Time is money. My wife has been dead two years—not quite, but for the sake of round numbers we'll say two. And I didn't know it was possible for me to love again, but there is a destiny that ties up our fag ends. And if you will . marry me, all my possessions and the eternal and grateful affections of my daughter Sappho shall be yours."

" I don't want any one to love me," she replied, without an accent of distress, calmly looking at him. " The less any one loves me the better I feel; I am afraid to be loved. And I couldn't marry you, Mr. Adams."

" Commodore Adams," he corrected her, bowing with a dignified resentment. " Even when the affairs of the heart are concerned we should not brush aside the delicate amenities of society. Commodore Adams, Miss Rose."

. " Pardon me. I lost sight of your title; I remembered only that you were a man seeking to express his love." There was no mischief on her lips, nor in her voice, but her eyes were laughing at him; and the merriment was so delicate, so spiritual, that he saw it not.

"Now, that ain't bad," he said. "Looking at it from my critical standpoint I should call it first-rate. But you won't marry me. Miss Rose, although a man of heart, I am, as you know, a man of business. You have declined my proposition and I hereby respectfully withdraw my affections and beg of you to forget that they were ever offered. I have raised your salary, but we'll let that stand. Don't think of quitting my employ, for I am still your friend. I am peculiar in my estimate of women, but I know them. Now, there's Ellen Avery, smart, bright, lady-like, pure-minded—but that's all there is to her."

"Well, what else could there be to any one?" Rose cried, laughing, almost shouting, in her mirth. He looked at her as if charmed by strange music. She sat down at her desk, still laughing, and bowing to her he felt about for the brass anchor that he wore on his cap.

"I hope I'm not interfering with business," he said. "But I fear that I am, so I will bid you good day. If any important matter comes up, you may send for me.

And this was her first romance on the Suwanee river. When the Commodore went out with his droll and whimsical countenance her mirth was also gone, and she sat with her arms on the desk, serious, thinking, troublously dreaming over what had been, wondering what was to be. And tall, strong, handsome in the glow-light of her fancy, stood the preacher. To her how strange it was that the pulpit, the soft and effeminate pulpit, should put forth a hero. Her nature, laced about by the finest nerves, looked with admiration upon the rugged and the fearless; and this preacher was rugged and he knew no fear.

CHAPTER VI.

Darkness lay upon the land and the river was black, for the twilight was gone and the moon was not yet risen. Rose sat alone in her room. She had told the family that she was given to moods—hateful moods, she said—and she besought the members of the houshold to pay no attention to her sulkiness. It was an easy way to explain her fitful longing for solitude.

There was a tap at the door. There had been no sound of a step, no creaking of the old stairs, and Rose sprang up with a start. " Who is it ?' she cried.

" I could say it is I, but I won't. I'll say it's me."

" Oh, come in." Rose sat down and Ellen entered.

" Why are you here all alone in the dark; shall I light the lamp?"

" No, the moon will be up presently."

" Let me sit down over here by you." With her foot she found a hassock, and moving it to the window, sat down, affectionately took Rose by the hand, and laughed with silly music. " Why, how cold your hand is, child. Why did you slip off up here alone? And you didn't remind me that I had something to tell you. How forgetful you are. But you might not have forgotten; you might simply not want to hear it."

" Oh, but I do want to hear it. Yes, I had forgotten."

" That was a crime. But if I tell you now, will you promise not to mention it to any one?"

" Perhaps you'd better not tell me, dear."

" Oh, now, that's the cruelest thing you could say. Promise that you won't mention it."

" Well, I promise."

" Thank you ever so much. It's the strangest thing you ever heard, and may be you'll think it's the most foolish. But it isn't foolish to me. I wish I could tell it just as it happened. But I know I can't—I can only try. Some time ago I was on a train not far from here. I had been on a visit North and was coming home. Well, when within about sixty miles of the place where I was to get off—the station where you got off—a man came along and in the gentlest voice asked me if he might share my seat. I looked up at him. He was tall and slender, had a soft, black mustache and big brown eyes. He wore a slouch hat, but he didn't take it off when he spoke to me, and I thought this was peculiar, but of course I didn't mention it. Well, before I knew what I was saying I told him that he might sit down. It was then just about six o'clock in the evening. He began to talk, and his voice was low and in it there was a wild sweetness. Darkness came on, and every now and then he would look at his watch, and he kept on looking at me, too, looking into my eyes. And oh, how he did stir me. He became silent, still looking at his watch. And then he talked poetry and he thrilled me. He asked my name and I told him—and I felt glad that I was privileged to tell him where I lived and all about myself. I told him that I hated common people, and this made him laugh. I knew that he wasn't common. I tried to find out what he was. He said that he wasn't a lawyer nor doctor nor any professional man. I asked him if he ever wrote poetry, and he said no, but that he liked it, the wildest and truest poetry. And then he looked at his watch. After a while he got up, and leaning over me he whispered, ' I won't do it.' ' Do what ? ' I asked. ' Don't be frightened,' he whispered. ' You are perfectly safe—everybody is safe on your account. Don't make any out-

cry, don't change your countenance. I am Haywood, the train robber. Hush!' He sat down
again, and now I was trembling. ' My men are
in the forward car and in a car behind, and on
the engine we have a man pretending to be an
engineer who went out on a strike. He once
belonged to the brotherhood and they don't suspect him. When I jerk this rope three times
the train will be stopped. But I won't jerk it.
You bring back the face of a sister whom I worshipped. At the next station, I will have my
men get off—I will tell them that I have discovered that there is not money enough on board to
pay us for the trouble. You may never see me
again, but in your gentle home I hope you will
remember that you have influenced the life of a
wayward man. I drifted into this—my parents
were gone, my sister was gone, and I became a
vagabond. I despised work, not because it was
hard but because it was common.'"

" I was crying now, and there were tears in his
eyes." ' Promise me that you will not do wrong
any more,' I pleaded, and the tears ran down his
cheeks. ' It is not the memory of wrongs com-
mitted that makes me weep,' he said. ' Your
soul draws tears from my soul. Good bye. I
will go back and see my men and send some one

forward when the train stops. I may write to you.' He was gone.

" The train stopped. I scarcely knew when I reached my station. Rose, I knew nothing except that the man had robbed one person on the train —robbed me of my heart. I came home and dreamed, and mother scolded. She wanted me to marry a man and I hated the sight of him. One day a letter came for me. And I trembled as I broke the seal. It was from him. He said that he could not stay away from me—he was in New Orleans, apart from his men. He begged me to let him come to see me. A reward was out for him—oh, Rose, why do you tremble so ? But I know it is affecting. A reward was out for him and he must come at night. He knew of our place, I had told him all about it, and he said that he would steal up the river at night and meet me in the garden. I couldn't refuse him— I didn't want him to rob people, I wanted to re-form him, and I told him that he might come. He did and I met him. Old Jude saw us to-gether and I begged him not to tell and he won't. He has been here four times. He was here last night, and he can't live without me, and I must go with him."

She put her head in Rose's lap, and the moonlight fell in at the window and the two girls were silvered as they sat there motionless and silent.

" Rose, what must I do ?"

" You can do your duty."

" What is duty, Rose ?"

" An infliction that other people put upon us. Do you really love this man ?"

" Yes, I worship him."

" Because he is a robber ?"

" No, because he is a man—I would love such a man even if he dug ditches for a living." ·

" Then marry him."

" Yes, but brother, and mother !"

" Your brother will approve of it, and your mother must. But be careful, Ellen. Listen to your heart, and remember that the heart can be indiscreetly fond. I was sitting here at the window and I saw you meet him—saw you stand together on the spot where the summer house sank into dust, and I knew that it was a new romance building amid the ashes of many an old one; but I confess that I was anxious and afraid that you were doing a wrong, not to others but unto yourself. Yes, marry him. Your surroundings and your friends would stamp me an evil counsellor, but our happiness lies not in what others think, but in what we *know*. I would rather have one day of joy with a robber than a life-time of mere contentment with a saint. Man says duty; nature says love. Man has looked for love and has told woman that she must hide from it. But a new woman is coming forward, not a lecturer, but a woman with a broader soul. I was a rebel at college; they were to teach me, but when they found me seeking a wisdom that lay beyond the knowledge put down in their books, they tried to reason me away from truth and independence, and I laughed at them. Afterward I confessed my love for the nude in art, and the vulgar said that I was immodest."

"Go on and tell me more about yourself," Ellen pleaded, sitting up and resting her arm on the window sill. "Why did you leave the world where you could do so much and come here to work in a miserable office? If you must work, couldn't you do better in the North? Women have no chance here."

"I can't tell you any more about myself, dear. But I want you to know this—I am truthful just as far as I can be."

"But have you ever loved an outcast?"

Rose laughed, drew the girl toward her, kissed her. "Perhaps I might be happier if I had," she said.

" But, Rose, I have told you my secret, because I knew it would be safe with you. Now tell me yours—you have one; please tell me."

" Little girl, you told me yours because you couldn't keep it. Don't urge me; let us sit here and dream."

CHAPTER VII.

There came another tap at the door, and this time the preacher's voice was heard. "It is a crime for you girls to shut yourselves within doors such a night as this," he said. "Come and let us float down the river." Rose asked if it were not too late, and laughing he replied that tide and not time was all that had to do with it. Ellen declared that she could not go. "No, I won't go through the garden at night. Afraid? No,.it's a sentiment with me. You and Rose may go."

They did not urge her. At the bottom of the garden they got into a boat and floated away. The coming of scents from the woods was all that told of a breeze stirring. The water was calm, appeared not even to flow but to rest in the moonlight. From far away came a negro's melancholy song; down below, somewhere on the island, a mother was singing her baby to sleep. Avery did not even guide the boat; he simply let it drift. Once it touched the bank, slowly turned round and drifted off again. He said that it was pleasant not to know whither one was going, planning spoiled the pleasure of a surprise. They passed under the low boughs of the live oak, and from the dark, looked out upon the gleaming light. At a place where there was no bank but a marsh, they drifted into a bed of lilies and the boat was still.

" Are you going to shove it off?" she asked.

" Yes, after a while. Let us rest here where we can see so much." He was silent for a few moments, looking about him, and then he added: " What need of a pulpit when we can have such a scene as this? Rose, I never thought my calling narrow until time and again you reminded me that I was a preacher. I see now that it is narrow, and I am going to give it up."

" No, you must not," she replied, almost fiercely. " It is a duty you owe your mother."

" What, to be a hypocrite? And without hypocrisy I can't preach as they want me to."

" Yes, you can; you can preach the gospel."

" No, not as they would have it. Their gospel is narrow; mine is anarchy. I am an anarchist; Christ was an anarchist. I don't mean against law, but against religions. Let me shove off."

Again they were afloat. " For one I love I would be a hypocrite," she said. " Wouldn't you?"

"I don't want to think so, Rose. And yet I
wouldn't hesitate to say that I would go to the
deepest hell for one I love. But duty doesn't lay
upon me with a compelling heaviness. Have
you ever tried to think that everything is for the
best?"

"I would despise myself if I thought so," she
replied bitterly. "I worshipped my father, and
death took him and that is the reason I sometimes don't like God."

"Rose!" he cried.

"I ask pardon for that," she quickly added,
even while his voice was ringing in the air. She
looked upward, and dipping a handful of water,
she poured it on her head.

For a long time they were silent. "The day
after to-morrow will be Sunday, and then I will
preach a sermon that will put me out of the
church," he said.

"Please don't," she pleaded. "Think of your
mother."

"Don't tell me to think of any one. Let me
think of whom I must. We turn here to row
back."

It seemed that the girl's mood changed with
the turning of the boat. She talked with careless and childish gaiety, breaking one sentence to

begin another; she threw handfuls of water into the air, and laughingly cried that the glittering shower was a blizzard come down from the stars. Avery could but gaze in astonishment at her. Where had she put her melancholy dignity?

"You are an irridescent creature," he said, slowly pulling at the oars. "You inspire a thoughtful sadness and then you laugh at it."

"But if I do neither by design I am not to blame," she replied, rippling like the water at the bow of the boat. "If I had my way I would make every one happy. Is that an owl hooting at us? Yes, it is, the impudent creature. What a pretense that bird's life must be; shouting his dullness; hoarse with dignity; and he would have us believe that he is wise. How like a man— some men, I mean. How natural it is that the stupid should be dignified. But you are not dignified, Mr. Louis. You are what the girls would call so nice. Why, there is a log drifting down, and the water is not high either. I won-der where all the drift wood comes from."

"It must come from up the river," he replied.

"Really!" she cried, throwing a shower of water about him. "Why don't you advance that as a newly conceived theory? I shouldn't wonder but it might be accepted. Why, here we

are, almost at the garden; I didn't know you
were pulling so hard; didn't suppose you were
so anxious to get back."

" Shall I let the boat drift again?"

" Oh, no, it is time to get out.' Oh, I have en-
joyed this *so* much, Mr. Louis."

He helped her out and was chaining the boat
when they heard the quick dipping of oars. From
a black shadow a boat shot into the light, and
made straight for the garden.

" Rose, go to the house and I will see what
this man wants."

She hesitated; she feared the man might be
Ellen's robber. " Don't you think you might as
well come too?" she asked. " It isn't likely that
he wants anything."

" Are you afraid to go alone?"

" No; what a question. I'll go. Good night,
Mr. Imperative Mood."

He turned to detain her, but she ran away
childishly laughing.

A man got out of the boat and stood on the
bank, looking about him. " Is that you, Andrew?" Avery asked, starting toward him.

" No," a voice answered. The man came up
the bank to meet Avery.

" May I ask who you are and what you are doing here?" They were now face to face.

" This is Mr. Avery, I suppose.   It makes no difference who I am.   What I want is the question."

" Then what do you want, sir?"

" A woman.   Mr. Avery, you are a minister of the gospel and a man of justice.   Therefore I will tell you why I want a woman.   I don't want to create any sensation; I want to do my work quietly."

" Who are you, sir?" Avery demanded, leaning forward to search his face.

" I am an officer of the law, and I am from down the river.   I don't want to disturb you, but I must tell you that under your roof is a woman that I must take away.   I have a requisition for her."

Avery staggered back, but stepped forward again and stood hard on the ground, gazing at the man.

" Explain," he quietly said.

" I will, and I hope you'll appreciate my motive in coming here at night.   The beautiful woman in your house is Rose Grayham, and she is wanted in Colorado—wanted for the murder of a man named Powell.   There is no question of her guilt; she was seen to kill the man—blew out his brains.   The governor of the state has offered

five hundred dollars reward for her, not a large sum, but Powell was not a very prominent man. I discovered her, and I want the reward."

Avery stepped closer, put his hand on the man's head, turned his face toward the moon. "I want to see your countenance," he said, gazing upon him. "I want to make a study of your infamous face. Don't you move; don't take your eyes off the moon while I am talking to you. Oh, you villainous off-scouring of the earth! You have heard of me; you know that I am afraid of nothing that walks the ground; you know that I will keep my word; and now let me tell you that if you go to the house or in any way show yourself to that woman, I will cut your throat. Do you hear me?"

"Yes, Mr. Avery, but justice—"

"Justice be damned. If you look at her, I will cut your throat. Give me the requisition."

Avery took the paper, tore it into bits, and threw them into the river.

"Does any one else know of this?"

"No, sir; no one but the people at the State House who issued it."

"Don't look at me—look up there. You write and tell them that you were wrong, and don't you breathe a word to any one else. You care nothing for justice—you want the reward. And I will see that your base soul is not cheated. From the church here I receive one hundred dollars a month, and every month I will give you fifty dollars until five hundred are paid. On the fifteenth of every month, at twelve o'clock at night, meet me here. Are my terms satisfactory?"

"Perfectly, Mr. Avery. I don't want to run against you. My name is—"

"Hush, wolf, don't howl your name. Go now, and remember that if you whisper one word, or that if you come to this village except at midnight on the fifteenth of the month, I will find you, follow you, and—you know what. There's your boat."

CHAPTER VIII.

Avery stood and watched the fellow's oars lashing in the light, the devil throwing kisses at the moon, he mused, as he turned away. To the ruined summer house he went and down upon the ashes he sat, with his head in his hands, with his heart in the dust at his feet. The hours passed, but still he sat there. Morning came and the birds fluttered in the bushes about him. He looked up and the sun blazed on his haggard face. A worm, stiffened by the dew, warmed itself in the light and crawled away, and he looked after it until it was gone into the grass. The breakfast bell was rung, but he moved not until he heard his mother calling him. Then he went into the house. She gently reproached him for having got up so early when he might have been drawing strength from the sleep that comes at morning. On the following Sunday the people expected a great and soul-satisfying sermon and he ought not to put himself to the risk of disappointing them. And at the breakfast table when Ellen told her that his bed had not been disturbed, she distressfully scolded him. She knew that he was going to break himself down, and her heart was so set upon his pulpit work. She harassed him with a needless show of solicitude, with an affection in which he saw too much pride, and from about his neck he took her arms and told her to sit down. She whimpered that he cared nothing for her love, and he replied that he loved her but that she must not be foolish over him, must not be proud of him; said that all pride was selfishness. Rose came into the room, and her beauty, her freshness startled him. Over her he had pondered during the night, pondered until his fevered imagery had blurred her countenance, and he hoped at morning to find a repellent flaw in her face, an evil light in her eyes, but she was beautiful and her eyes held an entrancing glow.

"Mr. Louis, are you well this morning?" she asked, laughing; but her voice saddened as she glanced at him. "Oh, you have been worrying," she added. "The man who smoothes out the worries of others should not distress himself. I wish I didn't have to sit in that office to-day. I want to go away down the river where the vines are so tangled. Won't you take me down there some time, Mr. Louis?"

"We shall visit many places one of these

days," he answered. " Nothing is more inspiring than to see innocence gazing upon nature."

" Don't be sarcastic, Mr. Louis. He went to battle with what he called my reserve, and conquered it, but now he is sarcastic. But I will excuse that, Mr. Louis. Remember, sir, that you have promised to preach an orthodox sermon to-morrow. I am going to sit close in front and shake my fist at you if you depart from the faith."

" Thank you," Mrs. Avery spoke up. " You don't know how much good it does me to hear you say that. And you *will* preach an orthodox sermon, won't you, Louis ?"

" I shall leave it to you whether I have or not," he answered. " When the sermon is done I shall accept your opinion."

Rose was worried as she walked toward the office. Avery had said that he would preach a sermon that would put him out of the church, and she believed that he would keep his word. But her spirits were lightened by the soft charm in the air; she was willing to leave it all to chance. Everything she looked at was a delight to her, the dew slowly dripping from the hanging moss, the bird fluttering in ecstasy as if he had found a new song. Men were already

sitting in the shade of the tavern, old fellows full
of good humor, amused at everything and yet too
deliciously lazy to laugh. The mayor saw Rose
coming, got up, put on his yellow linen coat and
joining her, walked toward the office with her.

" I want to talk to you about a very serious
matter," he said. " I might almost say that it is
a mighty serious matter, Miss Sibley, or Miss
Rose, as everybody is beginning to call you.
Yes, I want to talk to you about a very serious
matter."

" How can you on such a morning as this ?"

" Ah, but why this morning more than any
other ? Nearly all mornings are the same here."

" No, sir, this is the brightest and sweetest
morning that ever was; last night was the
sweetest night that ever was, and to-day I'm
going to do nothing but gush. So don't talk
about anythiug very serious."

" I really wouldn't, now, Miss Rose, I pledge you
my word as an official and a gentleman I
wouldn't, if it wa'n't right directly in the interest
of society. We've got to make sacrifices for
society, you know. It's this way, Miss Rose:
We are all might'ly attached to the good and brave
brother Avery; we all acknowledge that he is
about as game a man as ever came over the dirt

road, but bravery don't always conserve the best interests of religion. He is about as smart a man as anybody ever heard preach, but," he added in a loud and significant whisper, " he's a-getting a leetle too far off the track. It's all right to wabble, you understand, but it ain't all right to git off entirely. I won't say anything about myself, for I can stand almost anything, but the majority of our people want their religion served up as hot as a fresh hoe cake. And brother Avery don't seem to understand this. He stands up there, tall and grand like a born orator, but he don't jolt 'em often enough. The truth of it is they want hell fire and a heap of it. Why, what's the use of having an enemy if there ain't no hell for him to go to, hah? He ain't treating us right, you see. He don't frown hard enough on sin. So to-morrow they are sorter going to sit in judgment on him, and as I am his friend, I wish you'd kinder drop him a hint."

" Why don't you do it?" she asked.

" Well, now, I've been so busy that I hadn't thought of that. It rushes me mightily here to keep things straight. Let me see, I don't believe I want to inention it to him. He's mighty peculiar. Well, hope you'll pardon me for mentioning so serious a matter. I must hurry on back, now."

She looked round just before reaching the office, and saw him leaning against the tavern with his yellow linen coat hanging on his arm.

The Commodore had not yet arrived, but Sappho was sitting in the office, languidly fanning herself.

"Oh, so delighted to see you this morning," she said as Rose stepped into the room. "Moved by an inspiration, I got up early and went forth to kiss the dark and trembling Egyptian lips of the dawn." She made a note of this as Rose sat down, and her pea-eyes glittered over the record. "I am writing a drama," she went on, "and last night I charmed father with the first act."

"Have you seen many plays?" Rose asked, arranging the papers on her desk, giggling to herself.

"Not many of the rude and vulgar presentations that infest the stage, but I have reveled in the heroic play of nature. Oh, you look so sweet this morning; you come as the embodiment of the morning's dew. What did I do with my pencil? Here it is. I am so unbusinesslike that I fancied I had lost it." Again she scribbled, and then she added: " So glad you are with us, for you are so inspiring, so gentle a check on father's heedless methods. Where were you born, please ?"

" In a far distant place."

" Oh, how nice to have been born in a distant place. I was born in East Tennessee, and the thunder rocked my cradle, and the lightning dancing on the wall taught me the letters of the alphabet."

Rose turned and looked at her. " That is not bad," she said. " You have a riotous fancy, and always playing, it must play well at times."

" I don't know that I catch your meaning, dear. Fancy always playing must play well at times. Oh, yes, when it plays upon the soft sward of inspiration. Do you know I believe you could write?"

" And I surely believe you could, Miss Adams, if you were trained."

" Oh, I thank you for your frankness. You are the only one who has ever been frank with me. Won't you please tell me of my faults."

" No, I have too many of my own."

" Oh, thank you so much for the confidence you repose in me But I'm sure you have no faults; a beautiful woman never has. There, now, I have been too frank. Won't you please pardon me? I couldn't help saying it. You don't know how dreadfully tiresome it is to be un-attractive, do you?"

She fanned herself, sighed, looked to Rose for a compliment, and, of course, she got it. " You are not unattractive. You are graceful and—"

" Oh, do you really think so ? But surely you will be frank with me when I am so frank with you. Frankness is a charming quality. What does Mr. Avery think of me?"

"I don't know, I'm sure," Rose answered, looking down. " He rarely expresses his opinion of any one."

" Really? An odd man, isn't he ? Why, here is father."

The Commodore came in, blowing. He threw his cap on a table, ran his fingers through his dyed hair, bowed to the ladies, sat down and leaned back against the wall.

" Whew ! I'm rushed nearly to death. No wonder the foreigners make fun of us when we are such rip-snorters. Whew ! Been racing around all day, trying to corner a man."

" Oh, father ! " Sappho exclaimed. " Oh, how rude."

" My dear daughter, pardon me. I am dis-
traught—worried. Wonder what time it is.
Don't think I've wound my watch for a week.
Been so wretchedly busy. Pardon me. My
daughter, will you please retire to yonder corner? I wish to ask Miss Rose a question."

" Certainly, father. Your command comes
with the thrill of one of my own impulses."

She went into the corner and stood with her
face to the wall; and the Commodore leaning
over, whispered: " Did a man named Collins
want to look at that fifty acre tract up the river?
S-h-e-e—be easy."

" Yes, I think so. A man came yesterday—"

" Sh-e-e—same man. Reckon we've made a
sale. Sappho, you may come back now, dear."

" I thank you, father," she replied, turning
about, and with a limber swing she slowly ap-
proached her chair. " I shall sit here for a short
time and then I must go. My paper is itching
and must needs be scratched. And oh, will it
not be a glad day when my drama is completed?
And yet it will be sad, so sad, to see my dear
personages walking out of the sanctuary of my
confidence to seek the approval and the plaudits
of strangers."

She sighed with distressful languor and looked

upward. A shaggy dog that had been thrown into the river, came into the room, deliberately walked up to Sappho and shook himself. "Oh, father, do you see this impertinent monster? Go out of here. Oh, if I could be harsh with anything I would scold you."

"Git out!" the Commodore stormed. "Git! Belongs to a fellow named Collins that wants to buy land from us."

"Oh, father, how can you!"

"Pardon me, my dear daughter. I forgot. Men say that I have a smooth tongue, and how natural it is that anything smooth should slip up occasionally. My daughter, pardon me, but I am expecting some men on business, and in the impetuous whirl which may follow, some unpleasant things might be said, therefore, I opine that it would behoove you to retire."

"Into the corner again, father?"

"My daughter, the echo of the whirl will doubtless penetrate the recesses of the corner. Therefore seek the safe retirement of your home."

She arose without replying, bowed, and withdrew; and the Commodore, leaning back against the wall, gave his senses to the soothing influences of a nap.

New birds were coming from far up the river, and Rose sat watching them. The brighter ones, vain little creatures, paused by the water's edge to preen themselves, while the soberer ones were loud in their clamor against so senseless a frailty. The mayor and the town council, carrying their linen coats on their arms, slowly filed past to eat a Brunswick stew, prepared by a politician and to be served in a neighboring grove. The dull tramping of feet aroused the Commodore.

"Eh, what's up?" he asked, looking out. "Ah, those fellows are going to eat, and if I wa'n't so busy I'd go with them. Heigh ho!" He stretched himself. "Don't suppose you've changed your mind about what I said to you. You see how gentle I am with Sappho. I would be gentler than that with you."

"Mr. Adams—"

"Commodore, Miss Rose."

"Commodore, just at present I don't want to leave this place. I have found a contentment here that I might not find elsewhere; I have come into a new world, and to me it is soothing. And I don't want to leave, but I will if you ever speak to me again on that subject."

"Now, don't cry. I won't say another word

I swear by my landed investments that I won't. Can't afford to lose you—business would go to smash. Believe I'll go over yonder with them fellows and eat; want to eat right now."

CHAPTER IX.

In his study the preacher sat, meditating upon his sermon. During an earlier hour he had sought to sleep, but had failed. To close his eyes did not shut out the light. In horror he saw a face turned toward the moon, and the throbbings in his ears were the sharp and uneven accents of words spoken to a sinking heart. His mother had brought him a cup of tea. "Woman, please take that away." He saw the cup shaking in her hand and quickly he added, "Mother, I mean. I didn't know what I was saying But please take it away."

And now he sat with his text in front of him. Three times he had written it and each time the words had slowly faded from his sight. He looked into his own breast, searching for the love of the Galilean, and therein he saw a cross but no Christ. He dropped upon his knees, and clinging to the leaf of his desk as if it were a rock, he prayed with desperate fervor, but the cross was bare, and the nails driven into it were rusty. " Gone!" he cried; " gone, and in His stead is set not even one of the thieves but a murderess."

He got up, and shaking at the knees as one weighted with a great load, he went to the window and looked out upon the garden. A glare lay upon the ruins of the old summer house. He turned his gaze down the river toward the island, past the island, beyond the marsh where the boat had rested among the lilies, onward to the bend where glittering heat danced over the stream. He had often stood there to muse in fondness over this scene, at morning when the light was growing strong, at red evening when night could be seen sombrously stealing along the low banks; and in this contemplation he had found a worship. But the coming of another day had changed it al The same objects, indeed, were there, but they had been stripped of their spiritual vestments. And the desecrator had come up the river in a boat, in the moonlight. In his mind he forced the scene, the atmosphere of the night before. He saw her in the boat, saw her quickly baptise herself to atone for an impulsive blasphemy. He saw her mood change and he saw her spirits rise, heard her laugh, and he remembered that this change had come upon her at the exact moment when he acknowledged within himself that he worshipped her.

In his heart he could find no doubt that she had killed a man.   Love does not cast out fear; love invites fear; fear is love's companion.   Love is a ready judge; it sifts no evidence.   It takes the worst witness and cross-examines him.   From some neglected and forgotten corner of his conscience came a faint cry—duty.   He turned back into the room.   What was duty ?   Duty to whom ? To Christ ?   Christ was gone.

On the stairway there was a merry laugh, and to his heart his blood flew with a stab.   Rose had come home.   He heard her singing as she went into her room.   He tore up his text and went down stairs, went into the parlor where Ellen was singing.   The thought of the garden made him shudder.

" Oh, brother, you look so tired," said the girl, breaking her song.   " Haven't you been able to sleep any ?   Have I made so much noise ?"

He smiled at her; he heard that faint cry, duty; and he heeded it.   But what was his duty toward Rose ?   A man had wronged her and she had killed him.   He could forgive the murder easier than he could forget the wrong.   He smiled at his sister and he said: " I haven't tried to sleep —have been trying to work, but I can't."

" Well, let it go, why don't you ?   A sermon

that you have to dig out surely can't be your best work."

She sat on the piano stool, swinging her feet; she looked earnestly, almost distressfully at him and then said, looking down: " I ought to tell you something, I know I ought, and yet I don't know how."

" Don't try," he replied.

" But it may be something that you ought to know—something that you ought to have known long ago."

" I don't want to hear it."

" But suppose I am doing something that you could not approve of. What then?"

" If you are doing a wrong, stop; what you have done, keep to yourself. "

" Oh, but I can't stop."

" But you can keep it to yourself."

" What a changeable and funny old brother you are getting to be. Yes, I can keep it to myself and I will. I'll not force my confidence on any one, I'm sure. If you don't want to hear the most romantic story you ever heard, very well, you shan't; and after this you needn't ask me, for I won't tell you. I ought not to tell you, anyway, and I'm glad now I didn't. Come in, Rose."

He looked up, still hoping to find an objection in the girl's face, in her manner, but found none. She was dressed in white, and about her head, put on with an air of mischief, was wreathed a rose vine. She smiled at him, sat down near him. She had thought to tell him what the mayor had said, to warn him not to antagonize the rulers of the church, but his sad face smote her, seemed to beg of her not to put upon him an additional distress. She felt that a rebellion had arisen in his conscience and that he was striving to fight it down.

" Mr. Louis, have you been in the house all day ? " she asked.

" I don't know—yes, I believe I have. I have been in my study looking down the river."

" And did you see the beauty and the charm that is always floating there ? "

" I saw a black shadow creeping toward a boat," he answered, gazing at her.

" But you mustn't look for shadows, and if they come they will go away if you don't en- courage them to remain. Oh, everything is so bright that I had forgotten there ever were any shadows. Let us float down the river now, Mr. Louis. Ellen will go this time."

" The air is still too warm," he replied.

" Then shall we go in the evening ? "

" You and Ellen go, I'm not well to-day."

" I am sorry. You are worrying over something. But you will feel better to-morrow. I
could worry but I won't. I believe we sometimes
fight against happiness."

" I don't," said Ellen. " I look for it, I
steal it."

" You would do that even if it were self-rob-
bery," Avery replied.

" But when we take something we don't rob
ourselves," Rose said, smiling at him. " When
we lose we are robbed. Oh, hasn't this been a
glorious day? When I awoke this morning I was
glad to be alive."

" And haven't you always been glad that you
were alive ?" he asked.

" No, not always," she answered, slowly shaking her head. " I have seen the time when to
find myself alive was a disappointment."

He looked at her and thought of a face turned
toward the moon. Suddenly he was startled by
the hope that the wretch had brought a lie in his
boat. She saw the change in his face, and play-
fully she asked: " What were you going to say,
Mr. Louis ? You thought of something. What
was it ?"

" Perhaps I thought of you baptizing yourself.'

" Now, please don't tell Ellen of that piece of silliness.   It was nothing, Ellen.   I said something mean and then poured water on my head to take off the curse."

" That was nothing," Ellen replied.   " If I were to pour water on my head every time I say a mean thing I think I'd be drowned after a while."

Mrs. Avery came into the room.   " Louis, my son, you don't look at all well," she said, seating herself on a sofa near him.   " And you distress me so when you look that way.   Your father looked that way at times, and it did distress me so.   You need medicine.   I do believe catnip would help you."

He laughed.   A few moments ago he would not even have smiled.   But now he was thinking of that possible lie brought in the boat.

" I am glad to see you laugh, my son.   Still, it is not a laughing matter.   To-morrow will be Sunday."

And this was the thought that lay with restless anxiety upon her mind.   She was in a dread lest he might say something to wound the elders, the Pharisees.

" Don't worry over me," he said, getting up.

" I don't need catnip, dog fennel or anything else But I do need to get at that sermon   I feel better toward it now."

He went out, and they heard him slowly walking the floor in his room.   With one of her sudden and romantic impulses Ellen ran into the garden to sit and dream among the shrubs that grew near the ruins of the summer house.

" Rose, have you talked to him about his sermon to-morrow?" Mrs. Avery asked.

" No.   I have been afraid."

" But I wish you would.   He pays such attention to what you say.   He seems to be drifting away from me," she whimpered.   " But I know your influence is good.   I love him so, but I am almost helpless.   Dear, sometime won't you tell me all about yourself ?"

" There is nothing to tell, Mrs. Avery.   Let us talk of something more important—of your son and the church."

CHAPTER X

Rose was in the garden near the river when the church bell rang. She looked toward the house, to the right, and saw Avery walking alone along the road leading to the place of worship. At breakfast he had been in better spirits than he had shown the night before, yet she felt that he would preach a sermon that might send him adrift. But she had said nothing to him—the opportunity came, for she met him alone in the hall, but she shrank from it. And now she stood looking after him, wishing that she had begged him to be orthodox, to please his mother and his narrow-minded censors. The hypocrisy of such a course did not strike her. Mrs. Avery called her, and she went to the house.

The church was crowded, even before the mayor and the town council filed in. There had been so much muttering that every one seemed to feel uneasy. The mayor was nervous, the town councilmen were disturbed. The Commodore looked at Rose and nodded knowingly, and Sappho closed her eyes and sighed with distress.

The choir sang tremulously. It was, indeed, an anxious day in Gaeta.

The preacher's text was a set phrase of faith, "Ye must be born again." He began with exceeding care, sometimes throwing away one word to take up a better one. But suddenly he dropped his care and talked rapidly, as if his sentences were thrown out by impulses, by unpremeditated convictions. No sermon could have been narrower. He believed in a veritable hell; he said that children must be baptised to be saved from perdition. He was an orthodox fanatic, a Puritan crank. The Pharisees were joyous, and when the sermon was done, they pressed forward to congratulate the preacher. They had not believed that so brave a man could turn his back upon the true doctrine. The mayor hinted at a raise of salary, and, although this made several of the wealthier brethren wince, yet they continued to praise the sermon, even though it were a desperate risk. Mrs. Avery was happy. She clutched Rose's arm and whispered: "God bless you for helping to do this." Rose knew not how to reply; she could not understand it. Sappho brought congratulations to the mother. "Oh, it was a poem from Israel," she said. "I could sit and listen to it all day, it

was so charming. Father, come and shake hands
with dear Mrs. Avery."

They had been slowly moving, waiting for the
preacher, and were now at the door. The Commodore stepped briskly forward, but realizing his
unwonted and untimely haste, he finished the
journey with a dragging of his feet. " Howdy
do!" he said, shaking hands with the old lady.
" Didn't know whether I'd come to church to-day
or not, but I'm mighty glad now that I did. It's
worth a good deal to me, I tell you. Be something to think about during my rush this coming
week. Standing right up to the grindstone now
all the time."

Sappho looked a reproof. The Commodore
added: " I am not going to talk about business,
my daughter. Far be it from me to profane the
Lord's day or to wound your feelings. Here's
brother Avery. Shake hands with him, Sappho.
Give him a good grip. She's timid, sir, but
she's warm hearted. And now, accept of my
congratulations, too. Best sermon I ever heard
—stake my possessions on that. And here's
Miss Ellen, always skirting the crowd, eh ?
Charming oddity, I assure you. What a sympathy there must be between you and Sappho.
But come, my daughter, we must go. I am expecting a man—"

" Father, how can you ? "

" Oh, but not on business, my dear child.
Brother Avery, drop in and see me. Good day,
and accept my tnanks for your great effort.'

Mrs. Avery took her son's arm and turned him
about toward home. Each congratulation had
called forth another flow of tears.

" Louis, you have done my heart so much
good to-day."

" What are our expenses ? " he asked, paying
no attention to her remark.

" Why, my son, what makes you ask that
question ? "

" A spirit of economy, mother. And no matter how little we are living on, we must begin at
once to live on less."

" Why, Mr. Louis," Rose spoke up, " I thought
you said you liked the South because it is shiftless
and prodigal."

" Did I say so? I was not orthodox then.
But being a Puritan now I must save, for with a
Puritan you know that the saving of money
is almost as important as the saving of souls.
Indeed, it is pretty much the same thing."

" Louis, my dear," cried Mrs. Avery, letting
her weight down upon his arm, " how can you
talk so, and that, too, after having made us so

happy? Will you promise me not to talk that way? Will you? You have done something to-day that assures us of our home and our hap,-piness, so please don't let any one hear you talk that way."

"All right, mother, but I don't suppose it makes any difference what I *think*."

"Oh, yes, it does. You must promise me not to think that way."

"I'se er hobbl'.n' laung atter you," a voice cried, and, looking round, they saw old Jude. "Neenter wait; I'll ketch up. Yas, sah." He soon overtook them. "Yas, sah, neber yeahed sich er sermont in my life. Didn' you see me dar at de winder? Dar I wuz er swallerin' dem fine words like er duck er grabbin' up co'n. An' sometimes I had ter hol' up my naik, da come so peart. Mr. Avery, ef I could talk dater way I neber would work no mo'. I'd say, 'g'way fum yeah, plow, g'way fum yeah, hoe, I doan wan' no mo' traffic wid you—g'way fum yeah, fur I'se dun 'spired o' de Lawd!' An' you'se 'spired, Mr. Avery, sho's you bawn, you is. No man could talk like dat lessen ole Moses, an' Ligy is stand- in' right dar wid him, wid der han's on his shoul- ders. Nor, sah; an' ef you'll talk dater way ter me ever day, I'll work fur you an' woan charge you er cent. An' I'm already gwine fetch you some chickens fur whut you already dun said."

" Where are you going to get the chickens?' the preacher asked.

" Neber min'; er man owes me some."

" Don't you steal any chickens for me, Jude."

" Sah! Bless you' life, I wa'n't thinkin' erbout stealin'. Couldn' steal atter yeahin' dat sermont. Nor, sah; nor."

Upon arriving at home, Rose and Ellen went up stairs, leaving Avery and his mother in the parlor. To have remembered a happier time would have strained the old lady's memory. Louis stood on the hearth with his hands behind him; his face was almost fiercely grave—he looked not the dreamy administrator of a visionary estate; there was no quiet musing in his eyes, no religion, no rest; he stood staring, and when his mother spoke he started.

" My son, you speak of economizing. And you don't know how it pleases me. You are now heeding the instincts of the Pilgrim Fathers, your people. It grieved me to see you fall in with the easy and shiftless ways of these people; it is not natural to you, and it seemed a dissipation. And I am so glad that you are going to **turn back into** the true path. Economy is a righteousness in the sight of the Lord.   And we can invest our savings, can't we?   Let me see. What would be a good investment?   An orange grove, wouldn't it?   Your uncle sells fruit, along with vegetables, you know.   And you could ship the oranges directly to him in Boston.   But I would insist upon his paying promptly.   Brother Lyman is one of the most honorable of men, but he is slow.   Louis, you are not paying the slightest attention to what I say.   Louis!"

" I beg your pardon," he said looking at her.

" Did you hear what I said?" she asked, rocking herself.

" I don't believe I caught it exactly."

" Well, I was talking about investing our savings.   What do you think?   Don't you believe in the orange idea?"

" Mother, please don't worry me."

" Well, I want to know!   Can't I talk to you for your own good, my son?   Are you not dearer to me than you are to any one on earth?   Louis, where are you going?"

" Into the garden."

" Let me go with you?"

He wheeled about.   " Mother, I want to be alone.   Please don't be fretted at me, and please don't worry over me."

He kissed her tenderly; and slowly smoothing her brow, he looked affectionately into her eyes. " Don't worry over me," he repeated.

Alone in the garden he moved about, seeking the places where the vines and the shrubs were most tangled.   He sat down on a mound where a rotting stake had let a rank honey-suckle fall to the ground, and sheltered thus, he sought to think, but no well-formed thought passed through his mind.   Half-shaped phrases, single words were seized by his eddying fancy and whirled about, and there was one word that floated to the center and turned slowly around—hypocrisy.   It was of loathesome shape, and it sickened him. But suddenly it grew graceful and glowed with a soft light: Love was dappling it with etherial hues, purple excuses, pink virtues.   He got up, shook the old vine, and through the briars picked his way to the river's brink, and there he stood, musing more sanely.   Suddenly a thought tore through him like a flying splinter.   Perhaps after all she did not love him.   Her face was calm, she gave no sign of suffering, and to love was to suffer.   Love was not a happiness but a distress, an afflication. He might forgive murder, he could almost forgive her for the wrong done her, but he must hate her if she did not love him. If she did love him he could kiss the blood on her hands. Then came that sweet balm, that Christ-anointed doubt. Perhaps a thief had stolen a lie at night and brought it in his boat. Should he tell her of his love and thereby force a crisis? He raised his hands between himself and this idea and shrank back from it. He would wait. For what? He would wait until he had paid that scoundrel every cent of the reward.

They called him to dinner. The meal was served under an arbor, and when he sat down a withered blossom fell upon his plate.

" Well, I think that was mean," Rose cried, laughing. " I will get you a fresh one." She ran away, and returning with a dahlia placed it beside the shrunken bloom. " There," she said as she resumed her seat opposite him; " we have two sermons lying together."

" Two sermons?" he repeated, looking at her.

" Yes; one makes us happy and the other makes us sad, but by viewing both, we—Oh, I don't know what I intended to say."

" You were going to say that one teaches us not to be too enthusiastic, and the other warns us not to be too sad."

" I thank you for helping me out. That was kind. It isn't often that a man helps a woman out of trouble. Isn't it beautiful here? I could sit here forever."

"I would want some one else to be with us if I were to sit here forever," Ellen declared; "somebody that I know."

"Ellen," said her mother, "don't be foo .sh, child."

"But mother, I would."

"Yes, I know; but don't be foolish. If you hadn't been foolish you could have had some one else to be with you all the time, but you were foolish. I don't know how you came to be foolish, I 'm sure. My people were all steady, with an eye to business; and so were your father's, and I don't know where you get it, I'm sure. Louis, you are not eating a thing. I am so afraid that you'll break down. Won't you promise me not to break down? I do believe that cow will open the gate with her horns. Look at her. And the cows in this part of the country are hardly worth their salt, either. There, she's going away. Ellen, who was that woman that sat just in front of you—that old-looking woman in a young hat? Rather queer taste, I'm sure, but she did seem to enjoy the sermon. They have some of the queerest notions of dress down here. That cow's coming back. No, she isn't."

With a jolt of impatience Avery sat himself back from the table. And Rose laughed at him, but he did not smile. " You are as nervous as a woman," she said.

" There may be sex among flowers but not among nerves," he replied. " Mother, I am go-ing out for the afternoon. I want to be alone."

He strode away, and the girls laughed at him and called him a crank. This time he did not pick his way through the tangled shrubbery; he walked rapidly down the garden path to the river, got into a boat, and shoved out into the current, though the sun was fierce. Sometimes he rowed with impulsive vigor, as if anxious to reach a certain place within a specified time, and then, crossing his oars, he would simply float, giving no heed to the hour but thinking deeply. The boat touched the lily marsh, and he let it rest there. He took off his hat, caught up a handful of water, threw it into the air and let it fall upon his head. Suddenly seizing the oars, he shoved out into the current and again rowed rapidly, rounded a bend where the water hummed an echoing tune among the cypress knees. Away from the settlement the banks were wild with in-terwoven vines; and flowers, fierce in their vivid-ness, flashed where the sunlight fell. The river

narrowed and in places the trees on each side
leaned over and mingled their branches. And
now the current was swifter but noiseless. He
landed the boat where the timber was thickest,
and walked out into the forest. Under a great tree
he sat down on a log. The place was so still,
the air was so quiet, that he thought aloud.
" She is not suffer'ng, and therefore she does not
love me. Love is an agony. But why did
her manner change at the very instant I acknowledged that I loved her ? Can it be that she wants
me to love her ? Then why should she not love
with me ? I wonder if a man can turn upon his soul
and kill it ? It is better to have no soul. Oh, I
wish she would tell me that she murdered a man.
I could forgive her. But why did she murder
him; could I forgive the why ? No, animalism,
man, is too strong within me. If a man wronged
her, she loved him, and if she loved him, she
can't love me. She might have an affection for
me, but I would spurn that — I would hate
her affection. She must worship me; she must
give all that I give. If she were to come to this
place with me she would confess. This is a
cloister and I am a priest. A priest; I hate that
word. How much better it is to be a man,
a free man. God, but if I could be as free as I

was before I met that woman! By meeting her I was reduced to slavery and to cowardice. I will fetch her to this place."

Near by stood a dead tree, with two projecting snags far toward the top, forming a cross, and this cross was covered with vines. On the arm-pieces, near the ends, were blood-red trumpet blooms. He looked up at the cross, and to him it had not been formed by a whim of nature but by direct design. "I will fetch her to the cross and she will confess," he said, clasping his hands. "Moses lifted up the serpent in the wilderness, and here in the wilderness the son of man is lifted up."

He ran toward the river, ripped through the tangles, bounded over logs. He sprang into the boat, and keeping close to the shore where the current was not strong, tore his way up the stream. Just as the boat touched the bottom of the garden, he saw Rose standing in a path not far away. He called her, and quickly she went to him.

"Step in, please," he said, holding a shrub to keep the boat steady.

"Shall I call Ellen?"

"Won't you please step in? I have found a place that I want to show you."

She looked about her, toward the house, up the road leading through the village. " Why not?" she said, and with a laugh she stepped into the boat, and resignedly sat down. He shoved off, caught the water with a sweep of the oars, and the boat shot down the stream. His hat was off, and the sun was still fierce, but be let it beat upon his head. Suddenly she spoke, almost with a cry:

" Please don't look at me that way."

He put on his hat, glanced round to see if the boat were in the swiftest current, and then asked:

" How am I looking at you?"

" As you should, *now;* but just then you looked as if you were my deadly enemy."

" Have you met many deadly enemies?" he asked, forgetting a stroke, gazing at her.

" I remember one," she answered.

" Tell me about him. Don't say you won't. I must know. Tell me about 'im."

" Suppose I couldn't tell you about *him* but about *her*."

" Oh, a woman."

Then he saw her rival. A man had deceived her, had forsaken her for another woman. The man who had wronged her was not her enemy, but the woman who had won him was—she was

hated, he was forgiven, and she killed him because she hated *her*.

"You are about to look at me that way
again," she said. "Please don't. Why do you
worry so much? Is religion so burdensome a
load?"

"No, but hypocrisy is."

"You are not a hypocrite. You have simply
given the people what they wanted, and that was
a kindness; besides, you did it for your mother.
You are so brave and strong that I don't see how
you can worry. I had thought worry was mostly
a womanly affliction, and that when man took
it up he was stealing something from woman.
But there, don't let us talk about anything disagreeable when there is so much beauty spread
out for us. Oh, those woods are charming, Mr.
Louis, and I believe there are fairies among the
trees. That's silly, but you must let me be silly,
for when I am silly I catch the perfume of a distant happiness, coming toward me. And this is
foolish, I know, but I like to be foolish. I could
be serious, however, Mr. Louis. I *am* sometimes and then I am unhappy. But we don't
learn much from a serious mood, do we? We
are guarding ourselves then. Is it beautiful
where you are going to take me?"

" Charming," he answered. " There is a deep shade and an air that begs us for our secrets, and a vine-draped cross that almost demands a confession."

" Oh, a cross raised by the Spaniards, centuries ago? That must be charming."

" No, a cross raised by nature, no man knows when."

" You like to be vague, Mr. Louis. And I like you to be vague, too."

" Rose, tell me why you are so light-hearted. How can you be?"

" I can't be if you look at me reproachfully. I am holding up my heart, Mr. Louis. Yes, I have both hands under it. Why don't you hold up yours? I think I must have learned it from the Christian scientists, and although I tried it some time ago, yet it was a failure until recently. But I am not a Christian scientist. They look for contentment rather than joy, while I want to be insanely happy."

He looked searchingly at her, striving to find a flaw in her face, for upon a flaw he could have rested an encouragement. If a man be not vain, it is hard for him to believe that a beautiful women loves him. And Avery was not vain. If she loved him, why did she not fall into unison with his anxious and sorrowful mood? If he could only find some objection, something to criticize, he would catch it as a hope. But his eyes told him that she was faultless. Her smile threw a despair at him; the shape of her head, her hair, her voice, all were as testimony against him. But sitting on the log, looking at the cross, she might confess. What was it he wanted her to confess? That she loved him.

He landed the boat, helped her out, and led her through the woods to the log whereon he had sat.

" Sit down," he said.

" Wait till I get that flower." She plucked a bloom that grew on a tall weed, and then sat down beside him.

" What is it ?" she asked.

" A cross raised by nature."

" No, I mean the flower."

" I don't know, Do you see the cross? Look there."

" Yes, I see it. Beautiful, isn't it ?

" It is more than that. Does it stir any emotion within you ? "

" Yes, but it isn't any more wonderful than this flower. Both were reared by nature, and the flower grew on a weed."

"Rose, I really don't understand you."

"Why, what is there to understand?" she asked, reaching over and pinning the flower on his coat. "Isn't that pretty?" she asked, completing the work with a gentle pat. "Don't understand me?"

"No, I can't see very far into your nature. You perplex me."

"Then I am sorry. What bird is that with the red breast—looks as if it were hopping about with its heart exposed! Foolish bird to show its heart to the world, isn't it?"

She was not going to confess. He sat there gazing at her, wondering whether a serious thought of him lay on her mind. Suddenly there came a new fear, and it fell upon his heart with cold conviction. She was a flirt. Her heart had been ruined by a man, and now out of wantonness and revenge she would ruin the hearts of men. She was playing with him; he would play with her—he would lift up his heart and be lively of mood.

"I wonder that there is not an old mission near this spot," she said. "It is the right place for one."

"There are the ruins of one not more than a mile from here," he replied. "I stood there once and preached a sermon."

" One you felt, or one you thought people wanted ? "

" One that people wanted—the flattery craved by a self-righteous conceit and narrow souls. And that reminds me to preach a sermon one of these days that will lift my congregation off the benches. You must be there; it will be rare sport."

" Why, Mr. Louis, how can you talk so? That would shock your mother I should like to sit here longer, but it's growing late. Shall we go?"

" Surely; but with a regret that I have not given you a gayer time. Sometime we will come with a large party—bring some negro boys and let them dance under the cross."

They were walking along now, and she looked up at him; he thought that he heard her sigh, and he smiled at her. She had played him with prattle, and now she would play him with signs of distress.

" I wonder if the boat has drifted off," he said, now walking in advance of her. " It would be too bad to have you walk home. Ah, there it is. The sun is nearly down, but I will soon land you in the garden. Let me hold it steady. Now you're all right."

He shoved off with a song, a rollicking air,

whose echoes still live in the angles of old Yale. "Did you suppose I could row so rapidly?" he asked when the boat had crossed the current into the stiller water.

"No, and I didn't dream that you could sing with so sweet and charming a recklessness."

"Neither the song nor the recklessness is as sweet as your flattery."

"Oh, I didn't suppose you liked flattery, Mr. Louis."

"What, am I not a man, and is not a man a fool?"

When they landed at the garden the sun was down, and bee-martins were darting through the fading light. "Don't wait for me," he said, helping her out. "I must be alone for a time, to listen to a discussion between my conscience and my judgment."

CHAPTER XI.

The next day was cloudless, the air was just as soft as it had been the day before, the river was just as beautiful in its dreamy stretches below the town, the breath blown from the woods was just as sweet, and yet nothing was the same to the girl as she sat at her desk in the office. There was wanting an essence, a sublimation. The change had come the evening before, when Avery caught up his rollicking song. To her it had seemed heartless, a cruelty shouted upon the spiritual air of the twilight.

The Commodore came in puffing. " I've had a hard chase this morning," he said. " Heard that a capitalist had arrived, and I had to hunt him down. Miss Rose, the motto of successful business is, 'let no monied man escape' You may not realize this at present, but when you have been in business as long as I have, you will. And I think that my morning's chase will amount to something. He didn't say so, but I saw it in his eye. In business, Miss Rose, the lips may remain quiet while the eyes are shouting. **And**

I think it would be well for you to remember this."

He sat down in his accustomed place, with his chair tipped back against the wall. " Yes, the eye seeks to practice shrewdness, but by an expert it is easily detected. I have just heard that Avery's Swamp Angel will, on a change of venue, be tried over at Rampa. Good thing—removes an annoyance from this community. But I'd rather like to see him hanged, though understand that I don't want him strung up here; hurt business; give us bad advertising. Why, you don't look well, this morning; that is, you look well—always do that—but something seems to be worrying you."

"I am not feeling well," she answered.

"Sorry, but it *is* a little dull this morning. However, things may pick up pretty soon. Wasn't that a glorious sermon we had yesterday? Haven't been so edified since I heard my fleet chaplain discourse on the necessity of agonizing for the faith. And there's no danger of Avery leaving us now. It wouldn't be business to let him go. Sappho was charmed, and I want to say that when she's charmed, she's charming. But I've been worried over her of late, though this is strictly confidential. A sort of horse doctor has been coming to see her—fellow named Block. Now, some people might think it's business to have a horse doctor in the family, but I don't. And what worries me is that Sappho rather takes to him—calls him such a character. But I don't want any characters about me. A character is always an unruly thing, and my long schooling in the navy has given me a reverence for discipline. Well, I am so worn out that I may drop off to sleep, and if any important question arises, you may wake me."

He was soon asleep, and Rose sat there with the ribald notes of Avery's song ringing in her ears. A woman may be pleased with light talk and with a lively manner, but her respect for a man rests upon his seriousness, his ardor, for to her there is a charm even in an enthusiastic trouble. Avery had thrown off a trouble. She had told him to lift up his heart, but when he did so, her heart sank. She was still pleased to meditate upon his narrow sermon, for she knew that he had sacrificed his convictions, that out of reverence for his mother he had acted a distasteful part. And yet she feared that the very force of his resolve, the subjecting strength required to make the effort, had changed his nature. She regretted that she had shown him the light and playful side of *her* nature.

The Commodore slept until along toward noon, and then he awoke with a snort. " Any important question come up ? " he asked, looking at his watch.

" No, nothing has come up and no one has come in."

" They are giving us the go-by," he replied, stretching himself. " They say that times are growing better, but I don't see it. A year ago to-day I sold eight acres up at Rodney's bend. It is true that the land came back on my hands, but then the sale indicated business, and that's what we are here for. Why, if here don't come Sappho and that horse doctor I'm the most pronounced goat that ever chewed a rag. For your sake, Miss Rose—I mean that rather than have a row I'll treat him politely. Ah, come in. You catch us deep in the throes of commercial turmoil."

Willowy Sappho came in, followed by the " doctor." He wore a cap and a short coat; he wore boots with high heels; he was short, rather heavy, and his face was freckled. His mouth was broad and his upper lip was long. He bowed with a short " duck," of his bullet head. " Mornin', or evenin,' just which it is. **Glad to see you, Com., old hoss.**"

"Doctor Block, I am pleased to present you to Miss Sibley," said Sappho, leading him forward.

He snatched off his cap, and with the stiff brim, topped his head twice. "Glad to meet you—heard about you. Don't know where you're from, but I reckon I've been in your range—used to go everywhere with the races."

Rose merely bowed, and the "Doctor," turning to Sappho, said: "She has given me the Dick Deadeye—scratches me."

"Oh, isn't he a character!" Sappho cried. "And, Miss Rose, I know you'll like him when you are better acquainted. So original, so unexpected. There is a chair, doctor. Sit down."

"Don't want to set. Set too much git like old hoss here after a while—want to set all the time."

"Dr. Block, my name is Commodore Adams and not old hoss, sir."

"All right, Com., old hoss; no harm done."

"Oh, how humorously delightful," Sappho shouted. "Oh, what a delicious character—how unlooked for. Father, the doctor is going to take dinner with us. Won't that be charming?"

"He is welcome at my board," the Commodore replied, "but I don't want any old hoss in mine. It isn't business."

" All right, no favorites, give you a fair start—
no handicap. What time do you eat, Miss
Saph ? "

" Doctor, you must not call me that."

" Call 'em back—got a bad start. Don't give
me the bad eye." She was looking reproachfully at him.

" I forgive you," Sappho sweetly declared,
holding out her hand. With one finger he
touched her palm, and with the same finger
topped his forehead twice. " All ready and all
set," he remarked. " Shall we hull now ? Miss
Simkins," he added, bowing to Rose, " bid you
good day. Going with us, Com. ? "

As Rose was going to dinner, she saw a number of men crowding about the doorway of a
small building, and as she was passing the place
the Mayor came out and spoke to her. " We
have just sent for Brother Avery," he said.
" They've got old Jude in there, arrested for
stealing chickens. And he puts up a most
remarkable story—says that he stole them for
Avery, to pay for that sermon yesterday. Here
comes Avery now."

The preacher spoke to the Mayor, bowed to
Rose, and said: " Walk along slowly and I'll
overtake you."

She walked on and had not gone far before Avery caught up with her, and beside him walked old Jude, his knock knees striking together.

" Yas, sah, da had me in er close place an' I'se monstus glad dat you got me out. But I could'n' he'p takin' dem chickens, ter save my life I could'n'. Suthin' I doan know whut, tole me ter take 'em ter yo' house ter pay fur dat sermont, an' I jes' could'n' keep my han's off'n 'em."

" And you did a disgraceful thing," Avery angrily replied. " You outraged the law and insulted the gospel."

" Yas, sah, I reckons I did, an' ef you feels dat way erbout it I'se monstus sorry. I'se ez hones', sah, ez de 'jority o' men, but er pusson dat won' steal fur dem dat he lubs is got er good deal o' col' pizen in de heart, an' I kain't he'p but lub dem white folks at yo' house. I did'n' want de chickens merse'f; I raises all de chickens I wants."

" Then why didn't you bring me some of your own ? "

" W'y, dar would'n' er been no sackerfice in dat, sah. I would'nter been 'miliatin' myse'f er nuff. I knowed dat it wuz wraung ter steal an' I

wanted ter feel dat I had crucified de flesh in yo'
beha'f. Dat's de way I felt. W'y, all de w'ite
folks yeah knows dat I would'n' take nuthin' dat
doan 'long ter me, an' dat's de reason you doan'
hab no mo' trouble er gettin' me off. I b'lebes,
sah, dat no matter whateber you does, ef you
praises de Lawd w'ile you doin' it, w'y, it's right.
I know I'se cuis—I knows I'se hard ter un'erstan',
but I ain't mean. An' now ef you'se mad at me
an' won' furgib me, I'll go off down yander in de
woods an' put my head down on de groun' in
sorrer."

"Stop," said Avery, and he took the old man
by the hand. "You are more honest and more
honorable than I am, and I respect you."

"Time fur me ter git erway fum yeah now,"
the old negro replied; "time fur me ter git erway
w'ile dis yeah joy is in my heart. Good day ter
you, an' ter you, sweet lady."

Avery and Rose walked slowly along the road
leading toward home; and the girl wondered
whether he would boisterously break into that
song when they should reach a place where the
trees were thick, leaning toward the river. But
they passed the place in silence, and came out
upon an old field, grown over with sassafras and
dewberry vines.

" Did I act rightly in forgiving the old man ? "
he asked.

" You know you did.   It was noble on your
part."

" Thank you."   And after a time he added:
" You are not as lively and playful as you were
yesterday."

" No," she replied; " and you are not as musical."

" Not as musical ?   Oh, you mean that foolish
song.   That meant nothing but a mood, and to-
day I am sadder, and therefore more sensible."

" Are men always sad when they are sensible ? "

" I don't know, but I think they are always
sensible when they are sad."

" I can't see the difference, but I won't worry
myself with looking for it."

He felt as they walked along, had felt since
the evening before, that she owed him some sort
of an apology.   He could not determine the sort
of apology it ought to be or why she should offer
it, but something was due him, some explana-
tion.

" I would rather see you lively than sad," he
said.

" Would you ?"

" Yes.   I thought that I would rather see you

sad, but I find now that I wouldn't. There is such music in a laugh."

" More than in a song ?" she asked, glancing at him, smiling.

" You are making fun of me now. But I can stand it. I have a shrewd idea of the ridiculous, and I know that I am ridiculous."

" If I thought you were serious I would protest against that remark."

" But of course I am not serious. I can't be serious when I am ridiculous."

" Please don't talk to me that way."

" I wouldn't if I thought you really cared."

She gave him a look of gentle reproach. He held the gate open and she passed into the garden, and without looking back went straightway to the house, to the arbor where dinner was waiting.

r.

CHAPTER XII.

That night when everyone else was asleep,
Ellen stole out into the garden. She stood near
the river bank, gazing down the shimmering
water-way. A bird, kept awake by the moon's
pouring light, sang on the top of a tree, but she
heeded not the song; she was listening for the
sound of oars, a more thrilling music. She was
waiting for her robber, and when the minutes
dragged by and he came not, she began to think
of the sin she was committing, thus to deceive
her mother. But it was a sweet and romantic
sin. She walked along down the bank to the
broken old fence, and then turning, went up the
stream until she came to a low brick wall, and
here she sat down to think. What could keep
him away so long? If he loved her, why did he
not come? She was beginning to doubt him.
After all, perhaps he had picked her up as a
mere fancy. Could a robber be honorable, even
with a heart? She would question him closely,
and if he were not honorable she would hate
him. She would make him confess that he did

not love her, and then she would despise him.
She caught at the faintest sounds, the strange
noises that float on a river at night, the rippling
of counter-currents that are not heard during the
day.   Suddenly she sprang to her feet, and ran
to the low bank where the boat lay.   She heard
the dipping of oars, and then a small craft
shot out of the shadow and came swiftly toward
her.

"Is that you?" she asked.

"Yes."   He sprang upon the shore, caught
her in his arms, kissed her.

"Oh, don't," she pettishly protested.   "Don't
do that.   You don't love me."

"Oh, you skeptic!" he cried, again pressing
her to his breast.   "You know I adore you."

"But that's so easy to say."

"Yes, for it is the truth.   Shall we go to the
old summer house?"

"No; over there to the wall.   Why are you
so late?   Didn't you know I was here waiting
for you?"

"Yes, and I got here as soon as I could.   I
broke an oar in my strong anxiety to get here,
and then I had to walk along the bank until I
could steal one out of somebody's boat."

She believed him; all was explained.   **She**

knew that he would not deceive her. They sat on the wall, and she fondly kissed him. "But you haven't told me how much you love me," she said.

"And I can't. If my love were water it couldn't flow through the channel of this river in a thousand years, and all the time the banks would be overflowed."

"Oh, how sweet that is," was her whispered cry, as she put her arms about his neck. "And will you always think that?"

"I will not always think it, but shall always know it."

"Oh, if I only knew. Teach me to know —compel me to know. And you never did love any one else, did you?"

"Never. I was once fond of a girl, but I never loved before."

"Fond of her? But I didn't want you to be fond of her—fondness is too close to love."

"This fondness wasn't, angel."

"Say that you simply liked her."

"That's all—I just liked her."

"But like is too close to love. I wish you hated her. You have seen her since you saw me?"

"No, I haven't."

" How long has it been since you saw her ?"

" More than a year."

" But you still think about her? Why should you remember her so long ?"

" I remember her because I can't forget anything. She is married now."

" Oh, and for that reason you have come to me. I don't like it. Why did you come all the way here to tell me about her? Why should you have thought about her?"

" Ellen, listen to me just a moment. You have reformed my life. You have made me a man. God left my soul unfinished, lifeless. You touched it, and it sprang up and shouted one word—love. And if I hadn't met you it never could have lived."

" Tell me that again," she whispered, with her head on his bosom."

He told it again, and for a long time they sat in a deep and sweet silence.

" Angel," he said, " I must soon take you away from here."

" I will go with you any time—now."

" No, not now. I would die for you, but I would not compromise your name. I will win the consent of your mother and brother and marry you in the house, openly, where every one can see."

"But the Mayor and the town council will come and arrest you."

" No, I will get a pardon from the governor. He is only too anxious for an assurance that I will quit the road—and the world shall know that you reformed me. I have already sent to the governor every cent that I took from the public. I slily went into a cotton speculation and made money."

" Oh, and won't it be heavenly to acknowledge our love to the world. I don't believe you ever wronged any one."

" If I did it was before you spoke the word of life to my soul."

Time, like a sparrow-hawk, sailed away. The moon went down, and along toward dawn the robber dipped his oars into the river.

CHAPTER XIII.

The next day was the 15th of the month, and the next night there was another scene in the garden. The sky was dark with clouds and the river was black. No bird sang in the tree, and the watcher who stood near the landing waited for no thrilling music. Rain began to fall, but he moved not. A wind came out of the black woods and whined in the bushes about him. The rain fell faster, but still he stood there. He heard the dipping of oars; he could see nothing. A boat landed.

" Anybody there?" a voice asked, coming cold and harsh out of the darkness.

" Yes, I am here."

" Then, I am in the right place. It's so dark I can't see very well. Can't we go some place out of this rain ?"

" No, come to me."

" All right, I can stand it if you can, I reckon."

He came up the bank and halted near Avery.

" Well, I'm on time. Always try to keep my

engagements. If you'll give me **the money, I'll** not keep you waiting."

" But I shall keep you waiting for a few moments. Tell me more."

" But can't we get out of the rain? I don't like this a little bit."

" There is no shelter at hand. Tell me how it happened—all you know."

" Well, you see, I am not thoroughly familiar with the details, but I'll tell you all I happend to have heard. This young lady was at a fashionable boarding house. And the man boarded there, too, as I understand it. It seems to have been a love quarrel. She was in the parlor at the piano when he came in. They were overheard talking loud, and then just as some one stepped to the door he fell dead, with his head almost blown off. I couldn't learn much about the man. It appears that he came from the East, from New Haven, I understand, and it was thought that he was there under an assumed name. I did hear that he was a tall fellow with light hair and—what are you grabbing me for? Look out, you hurt me. Let go my arm ! "

" That man I have reason to believe was my brother," Avery said, with strained calmness, liberating the fellow's arm. " An unfortunate affair with a woman drove him from home. We heard that he went to Colorado, and we knew that he must have changed his name, for we could find no trace of him. My mother believes that he is dead, and has rested her grief on an imaginary grave, away off somewhere on a mountain. But what do you care for this? Go on."

The fellow grunted. " Well, it is rather close now. I reckon you'd better let me take her and save your money. Look out, don't grab me again."

" Another suggestion like that and you'll go into the river."

" Wouldn't be much worse than this, Colonel, but I believe I'd rather take my chances here. Well, if there's no further business before the meeting, give me the money and I'll go. But how am I going to count it here in the dark?"

" Count it! You infamous scoundrel, would you presume to count it?"

" Oh, no, not if you object; still, it would look a little more business like. Let me have it, please. Thank you. I'll be back on time. Good night."

The rain fell faster, but Avery did not go to the house. Through the bushes and the briars he picked his way to the ruins of the old summer house, and there he sat down. He had taken the hand that had murdered his brother, and it had thrilled him. There could be no question, no doubt; she had slain him. But there was justice in her vengeance — he had wronged her as he had wronged a girl in the East. Why was there not in her eyes a trace of that murder? Why could he not find about her something to hate? But could he longer hope that she loved him? He said aloud that he hoped she did not, and he repeated the words, though he knew that he was a liar. He started to his feet; his mother was calling him. She met him at the door, stood there, holding a light.

" Why, my son, what on earth do you mean? I went to your room to see if the windows were down, and was so frightened not to find you there. And you are as wet as you can be! What on earth do you mean? Go right on to your room and I will bring you some tea. The water is still hot, I think. If it isn't I can heat it. Mercy on me! You look like a ghost. Something is worrying the life out of you, and won't you please tell me what it is? It's your duty to tell me, my son. But go right on up to your room."

" I shall, but please don't bring me any tea. I'm all right; nothing is worrying me more than usual."

She followed him with the light. " Look at all those flowers on the dresser," she said, entering the room. " Rose put them there this evening. She is so kind and considerate. I wa anxious about her at one time, but I'm not any more. You can't be any too fond of her now. She is so gentle and kind, and she seems to think so much of me. I will leave this light. I forgot to fill your lamp, I have had so much on my mind. No, your lamp is full. Rose must have filled it, for Ellen never thinks of anything. I will go now. Your underclothing is in the bottom drawer."

Avery lighted his lamp, sat down and gazed at the flowers. And she had put them there—the hand that had slain his brother had gathered them. He got up, took the flowers and put them out of sight, shut them in a closet. Then he changed his clothes, blew out the light, and went to bed. But he could see the flowers in the closet, could smell them. He turned over with his face to the wall, but the closet shifted and he saw the flowers, red and white roses—and their perfume came to him with a thrill. He turned upon his face, but in the black depths of his pillow the roses glowed. He sprang out of bed, seized the bouquet, tore it out of the vase, threw it from the window; but soon he was in the yard, groping about in the darkness - and the rain. When he returned he placed the roses on the dresser and sat near them, with his face against them. But suddenly he pushed himself back, dropped upon his knees and passionately prayed for strength. Lower and lower he bowed, in the acknowledgment of his weakness, until his forehead touched the floor. "O, God," he supplicated, "take her image out of my heart, let the blessed cross come back. I know that in Thy sight, yea, even in the sight of man, I am morbid, almost frothing the foam of madness, and I implore relief. If love is an insanity, hast Thou not made it so, for hast Thou not said that Thy name is Love! Merciful God, I know not what I am saying."

He sprang to his feet, seized the flowers, fell upon his bed; and when morning came, the roses were wet with his tears.

CHAPTER XIV.

Avery did not come down to breakfast. He told Ellen, who went to call him, that he had passed a bad night and that the only kindness that could be shown to him was to leave him undisturbed. Mrs. Avery knew that something ought to be done for him, furthermore she knew that he needed tea.

"Mother," said Ellen, "I should think that by this time you would have learned to leave him alone."

"My daughter," the old lady replied, giving the girl a sharp and reproving look, "it is hard for a foolish girl to appreciate the feelings of a mother. Is he not my son, the only son I have left!"

"But I'm your only daughter, too."

"Ellen, be sensible. There is a difference. You know that in all things we look to him. I'll go and see him and then I'll search old Dr. Gunn. He shan't lie there and suffer. He got wet last night and that's the trouble with him. Gracious me, it's a wonder that every man in the world isn't dead."

There were no clouds in the sky. Everything was fresh, and birds which yesterday had seemed dusty, now appeared brighter in new feathers. And yet, to Rose, the day had not recovered that strange deliciousness, that quivering essence of happiness, that had been left down the river. At the office she found the Commodore, already dozing in his accustomed seat.

" Come in," he said, looking up as she stepped into the room. " Oh, the lightest foot-fall stirs me this morning—I'm keen and alert for traffic. Closed a deal last night that has been hanging fire for more than a week—thought the gun was spiked, but it wasn't. And thus ten acres of land pass out from under my restless vigilance. You might write a short circular, embodying that fact; though, of course, you needn't mention the exact area of territory thus transferred. Had a sick horse at my house this morning, and although the profession which I followed so long inured me to scenes of distress, yet as a landsman I must say that I know of nothing more deplorable than the sight of a sick horse. But, fortunately, Dr. Block was present—having refused to take his departure, even after I intimated that he might do so with perfect propriety—was present and soon relieved the horse of all suffering.

And I must admit to you that this appealed to me, for to relieve dumb distress is one of the cardinal points of virtue. Yes, ma'am; and I thought to myself that I had no doubt underestimated the doctor. Still, I don't see how Sappho can admire him. Do you?"

"I ought not to say," Rose answered.

"Ah, but you could not admire him, could you."

She looked at him as if she knew not whether to laugh or to show resentment. "I could not," she simply answered.

"I thank you for the confidence which you thus repose in me, and I assure you that it shall not be abused; and now permit me to add that any other little confidences which you may be willing to extend shall be thankfully and respectfully received. Have you any others?"

"None whatever."

"Spoken too quickly for consideration. But tell me, what do you think of Mr. Avery? Take your time."

"I think that he is one man among a million."

"Spoken quickly, and therefore vaguely. Don't you think that he is peculiar?"

"I don't think that he is commonplace."

" Surely not.   And now, before I proceed further, let me say that I shouldn't like for him to
know that I have sought to discuss him.   Don't
want any misunderstanding with him.   Miss
Rose, it is a good—well, I'll call it moral scheme
—good, moral scheme, never to have any difference with an intense man.   As a type of man he
stands somewhat in an international attitude—he
belongs to all countries or to no country.   Don't
you think he is acting rather strangely of late?"

" Commodore, what do you want me to say?"
she asked, looking straight at him.

" Well, really, I don't know.   But I am sure
that I am prompted by an interest which I feel
for you.   A lone woman—"

" Nonsense!" she sharply broke in.   " That
lone woman idea is dead in this country."

" In the North, perhaps, but not quite in the
South.   Here a woman is still regarded as a
sentimental delicacy.   How's that for a piece
of offhand gallantry?   That's almost worthy of
my daughter, eh?   Sentiment is in our blood,
Miss Rose, just as flower seeds are in certain
wild patches of soil.   And there was a time
when poetry and feeling were appreciated here,
but even the South is changing.   Yes, we once
could sit about and enjoy one another's fancies,

but now everything is nerve-strung and hurried. Why, here's the doctor."

The horse-doctor came in, snatched off his cap, tapped his head, and seated himself on a corner of a table. " Glad to meet you again," he said, swinging one leg. " Some people I like to meet—some I don't. Miss Saph couldn't come; raked off an idea and had to put it down. Wonderful woman, Com. If she was to go to White Sulphur Springs durin' the hubbub she'd pinch the whole layout. I'd like to stay with you a few days, Com., but can't. Horses on the Peterson stock farm away up in Tennessee need my attention. But I'll come back again. Like this part of the country; somewhat out of the range of the high-flyers. No rich folks particularly, and you don't have to call everybody Colonel. Got any eatin', Com.?"

" Any what?"

" Any eatin' tobacco?"

" I used to chew when I was in the navy, sir, but I have given it up."

" All right, false start, call 'em back. By the way, I'd like to see you privately for a few mo ments."

" Why, yes," said the Commodore, looking about him. " Miss Rose, I don't think I'll need you any more to-day. You've been at work rather hard lately, and I think you need rest. Better go home, for I expect a pretty heavy strain to-morrow."

Rose did not stop at home, but passed through the garden and walked slowly down the river. She looked out upon the water as if she expected to find the essence of a sweet evening float-ing with the current; she sat on a pine log, op-posite the lily marsh, musing, listening with half consciousness to the sounds that came from the water and the woods—the splash of a gar, the mournful coo of a dove, the song of a negro, far away. Onward she walked rapidly, as if keep-ing step with a hastening man. She passed the island, came to the narrow channel where Avery had landed the boat; and now she halted, look-ing toward the vine cross, though the woods were so dense that she could not determine the place where it stood. She wondered whether that cross were her enemy, and believing that it had in some way changed her atmosphere, she gazed toward it with a feeling of strong and re-sentful emotion. Why should he have taken up a new and harsh personality just at the time when the old one had made her happy ? What would he have suspected ? That she was deceiving him? **She** was deceiving him, deceiving every one, but her deception lay not an inch beyond the line of self protection. She looked up the river and saw Avery coming toward her. Instinctively she put her hand to her eyes, as if to wipe out an expression that she did not want him to see. She turned toward him, as he drew nearer, and she saw that his face was flushed.

" Mr. Louis, why did you come out? You are positively ill; you alarm me. Come back with me at once."

" Are you going to worry about me too?" he asked, halting and gazing at her. " Please don't. I saw you through the window, and I wanted to talk to you. Do you believe I am insane?"

Swiftly she stepped forward and caught his hand. He sprang back with a shudder. " Not that hand, the other," he cried. " Give me your left hand. But wait. Are you left handed?"

" No, Mr. Louis?" she answered, trying to smile.

" Then I will take you by the left hand and lead you up the river. Come on. And I must slip into the house without mother seeing me. She must not know that I have been out. Your hand is cold."

" No, Mr. Louis, yours is hot. You have fever."

"Yes, but I am not insane. I haven't been well lately and I got wet last night—out in the garden, trying to think—not to think. Oh, your hand cools me, and my nerves are quiet. Look at those swallows skimming the water; they seem like thoughts flying about, bright in the sun and black in the shade."

"But graceful always," she said. "They are your thoughts."

He laughed, swinging her hand. They were two children. "Oh, wouldn't it be a glory to walk onward forever up the river, meeting no care coming down."

She smiled at him and there were tears in her eyes. "Unless we look for cares they some-times pass unobserved and unfelt," she replied.

"Little philosopher," he said, swinging her hand.

They halted to look at a bird's nest in a bush; they watched the heavy flight of a sand-hill crane; and again they walked onward, two chil-dren. But when they came to the garden fence he dropped her hand.

"Wait a moment," he said. "I am rational now, but I don't know how long I shall be. I know that you can keep a secret. You prove that every day."

"Please don't reproach me, Mr. Louis."

"I don't say it in reproach, but I know you can keep a secret. I fear that I am going to have a long illness, swamp fever, they call it here. But I have on hand a piece of business that must not be neglected. My salary will be brought by one of the deacons. I will tell mother to put it in my trunk, and you must get the key. You can easily do that. And at midnight of the fifteenth you take fifty dollars of it, slip out alone to the boat landing and give it to a scoun—to a man who will come in a boat. Tell him that you are my sister, that you know nothing except that you were told to give him the money. Don't let him talk to you—don't answer any questions. And as long as I am in bed you must meet him there on the night of the fifteenth of each month, and if I should die—"

"Mr. Louis!"

"Listen to me. If I should die, tell him that he shall have all his money as soon as the estate is settled. There is no estate, but you must tell him that, and then you must go away. Will you?"

"Yes, Mr. Louis, I will do anything for you."

He gazed at her and put his hand to his eyes.

"Don't you believe me?" she asked.

"Yes, I trust you. Now let us go to the house. Wait a moment—there's mother in the yard. Rose, I don't believe I can walk. I—" Slowly he sank to the ground. She dropped upon her knees beside him, lifted his head, kissed him passionately, desperately, sprang to her feet, and ran to the house. In the yard she found Jude. And the strong old negro carried Avery upstairs and tenderly put him to bed.

CHAPTER XV.

The community's leading physician informed the family that Avery was in great danger, that he had swamp fever in its worse form, and all forms were bad. Medical science, an explorer in nearly all directions, had failed to get at the inner nature of swamp fever. It partook of the complexion of yellow fever, but its decision was not so quick. Within a short time yellow fever declared a result, but swamp fever was whimsical and experimental, fraught with sudden turns, dawdling over one vital part then shifting to another. The patient might linger for months, with now and then a return of reason. The fever might leave him for days at a time and then come back. But one course was imperative; Avery must be taken to the hills, and the doctor suggested East Tennessee. Mrs. Avery acknowledged that the doctor was right. For a long time she had observed the slow but unmistakable approach of the disease. Her son's mind had not been clear, and old Gunn's book declared that mental cloudiness was a sure sign that a dangerous fever was not far off. She would go with her son. "And Ellen," she added, "you and Rose must board somewhere in the neighborhood. It won't do for you to live here alone."

"And why not, mother? Jude is here and could protect us."

"But it won't look well, my daughter. You must remember that these people have ideas of their own."

"And we will show them that we have too," Rose spoke up. "I don't care to board—I won't. I am going to stay here unless you positively order me to leave."

"And surely I'll not do that, my dear. I am really glad to see that you are so independent. Louis will get well—I know it, for it is my will and determination that he shall. His father had very nearly such a spell once, but he recovered. There is a fight on hand and I am ready, trusting in the Lord. It is no time to stand around and cry, and I am not going to cry until every hope is—is gone. Ellen, don't look at me that way. I'm not crying, anything of the sort, and you needn't say I am."

Avery was taken away, in an easy spring wagon, as far as the railway station, and thence in a sleeping car to the mountains. How dreary the old house was; how depressing was the air that first evening, when the shadows began slowly to creep in the garden. And when night came, Rose sat alone in her room, looking out toward the river. She wondered whether Avery knew that she kissed him, whether Ellen knew that she loved him. One moment she was warm and tremulously happy with the thought that Avery loved her; but the next instant she was cold and still with a poisonous doubt. If he loved her, why had he not told her? Timidity could not have touched him with its silence, for he was fearless both among men and women. Was it because she had withheld from him her confidence? But she could not tell him; he would not love her if he knew. She had striven to steal his affections. Calmly she thought of the danger of his dying, and a strength and a hope came out of the old lady's determined words. He might die, but she could even bear up under it if he should only send word that he loved her. She could see nothing beyond his love; she did not indulge a picturing of the happiness, the ecstasy that might follow; his love arose before her and dazzled all that lay back of it. Should she tell Ellen? No.

A purchaser called early at the office the next day and anxious to perform her duty, she closed a transaction with him, and the Commodore was snatched off the earth and shot into the upper air of delight.

"I don't believe I could have clinched it half as well," he declared when the customer had taken his leave. The Commodore walked up and down the room, making gestures that must have been a great tax on his energy. His cap was shoved back and his brass anchor was bright from recent rubbing.

"Sixty acres of land in less than half a day! Think of it—grasp it if you can. Not six acres, mind you, but sixty. Didn't we hit this community a jolt that time? Miss Rose, I promised not to mention a certain subject again, but your unexpected and hitherto hidden qualifications have put me to a severe test, and I am not going to prove faithless to the—well, task you have placed upon me, but you must permit me to remark that if our relationship were closer, sacredly bound, so to speak, why, we'd have money to burn; why, we would go down to the river and throw it in just for the fun of seeing it float away. There, now, I've had my say, and you needn't speak a word in reply, but I wish you'd think about it. Dr. Block was at my house again last night. Didn't go to look after the sick horse.

Can't stay away; and I don't blame him; for
when Sappho hits the humor she's a charmer.
Block refers to you as the thoroughbred—says
that if you were a race horse you'd be the finest
on earth. The idea occurred to me that I'd better knock him down for his impertinence, but I
considered his nature—it was the highest compliment he could pay a human being, so I took his
hand instead of giving him my fist. Sixty acres
in one day, and yet to look out there at that
quiet scene one might easily believe that nothing
of unusual moment had happened. Money to
burn. to smoke rabbits out of hollow logs, I tell
you! If—but I won't mention it. So they have
taken Avery away. And I want to tell you that
he's going to have a hard time of it. He's a power-
ful man and all that, but all strength is discounted
when swamp fever comes creeping out from
among the cypress trees and oozes into the
blood. Strongest man I ever saw outside of a
show was a fellow named Pitt. Whenever he
took hold of anything it had to stop. Well, he
went down to Bayou Margo to get out some
shingle timber, and the first thing we knew he
came back with swamp fever. They took him
to the mountains and all that sort of thing, and
he's up there yet, under a tree. Same way with

Bill Halpin.   As fine a fellow as you ever saw in your life, but—swamp fever."

" But why are you telling me all this?" she asked, picking up a pen which had just fallen to the floor.   She did not look at him.

" Oh, simply because it happened to come into my mind.   Man can't keep things out of his mind.   If he can he hasn't any mind."

" Have you ever known any one to recover from an attack of swamp fever?"

" Well, yes, I have, but it was a hard pull. Don't be alarmed, however.   I think Avery will come through."

He was now standing with his hand on the desk, looking earnestly at her.   " There is a chance.   But is there a chance for me, Miss Rose?   I beg your pardon for again referring to a subject which must indeed be disagreeable to you, but really I can't help myself.   Is there a chance for me?"

She looked up at him and her eyes were honest and frank.   " Not even the remotest," she answered.

" By which I am to infer," he replied, slightly shifting his position, " that you don't like me?"

" Not at all.   I do like you."

" But there is a stronger word.   You don't—

that is to say you don't—now I really beg your pardon for using a word which though at all times dear is sometimes presumptuous—don't love me?"

" I do not, Commodore."

" Ah, but you could learn."

" That has been said for ages.   But the love that we learn to bestow is the easiest love to take away."

" Ah, but it is sometimes held in so kindly and so strong a grasp that it can't be taken away."

" There is no grasp strong enough to hold a love that has been given as a duty.   Love is sublimely selfish; it doesn't take kindly to duty. Duty is a yoke and love wants a bow."

" Go on," said the Commodore, touching his brass anchor.   " Good streak you hit upon then; but I don't agree with you.   Love does know a duty and often it throws away the bow and nobly takes up the yoke.   Love is the same, no matter how attained.   The love that we learn to feel is just as strong, is calmer and often sweeter than the love that leaps out from an ambush and smites one.   It is none the less strong simply because we see it coming."

" But without a half frightening thrill love does not know its full deliciousness, and a plodding love can not thrill," she replied, looking at him.

"Ah," he rejoined, bowing and touching his anchor; "but a thrill is as likely to be a pain as a pleasure. And you don't think you could ever learn to love me?"

"I know I couldn't."

"But you have made progress since our last talk. Then you shut me off—threatened to go away, but now you calmly discuss the question."

She blushed and he leaned toward her, but the look that she gave him, threw him back, startled him.

"You don't understand me," she said. "At that time I did threaten to leave, but now I must remain."

"Until—" He gazed steadily at her.

"Yes," she simply answered.

He turned from the desk, walked to the door, came back, stood near her, and then said:

"I understand you. You don't threaten to go away because you have a duty to perform, and yet you say that love feels no duty."

She did not look up at him when she replied: "But perhaps in the hands of love duty is a sweet selfishness."

"Rose."

"Yes, sir."

" Some people think that I am one of the vainest and shallowest of men, and I admit that I am peculiar, but I am not shallow, neither am I unacquainted with the better feelings of this life. I admit that I am not well educated, but I have more than an average mind and I can think and talk fairly for the reason that I am a great assimilator.   However, using a vulgarism, I don't know but I am just a trifle cracked on the top of the head.   Now, after this confession, made in honesty, you are better acquainted with me, which leads me up to the asking of one question. Do you love Avery ?"

" Yes!"

" Does he love you ?

" He hasn't told me so, but I believe he does."

" Rose, I respect your frankness and will not violate your confidence.   And let me say, moreover, that I will serve you a good turn in every possible way.   Now, I promise you that never again shall you see a certain selfishness on my part.   I will more than ever be your friend. Avery is one of the noblest and bravest men that ever lived, and when I look at him, handsome and strong, I don't see how any woman could help admiring him.   IIe loves you—he can't help And I believe he will get well.   He has a good constitution, and nursing will bring him through all right. I never knew a strong man named Pitt to die of swamp fever; I have known many a man to get well. Sixty acres, just think of it! And yet the river refuses to flow up stream. I'm afraid you don't grasp it. Sixty acres in less than half a day! If you should see a bonfire pretty soon you may know that I am out in the street burning money. But you'd better go home now and stay there during the rest of the day, and if you don't feel very well to-morrow, don't come at all. Don't thank me; go right on. I've got to sit down here **now and try to realize that transaction."**

CHAPTER XVI.

The people of Gaeta were deeply anxious over the illness and the removal of their preacher. His vigorous return to straight orthodoxy, his declaration that there were infants in hell, had greatly endeared him to society. In the low lands of the South life may be inactive but religion must be intense, for into those dreamy waste-places filtered the sad and humiliated blood of the Puritan slave. Hither came the crushed Independent with chains about him, and here his children forgot their ancestry, but remembered their fathers' dark and sorrowful creed.

Rose and Ellen were objects of tender interest, and almost at any time they could look out and see sympathy coming down the road. Every day the old house was scented with flowers brought from the village gardens, and more than once did the Mayor and board of aldermen solemnly march down to ask if any information had been received from the mountains. Within a short time there came a letter from Mrs.

Avery. Her son had withstood the fatigue of the trip as well as any one could expect, but she dared not say that he was in any way improved, for the fever had not yet run long enough to have spent much of its force nor one-third of its determination. She had engaged an excellent physician, who, of course, assured her that the case was perilous to an alarming degree, though by no means hopeless. Her son had given no glimpse of returning reason; his mind was constantly wandering, sometimes along the river, sometimes out in a boat upon the stream. One symptom more than the rest had frightened her. He had, while raving, recanted from the strong faith so recently put forth by him; it seemed that some one was questioning him, and with contempt he snorted at the idea that there were infants in hell. She instructed that this part of her letter must not be made known in the village.

One night Ellen stood in the garden waiting for a boat. There was no moon but the stars were out, and in the Suwanee country the stars appear to be so near the earth, so very close that one feels a new interest in them. That morning the girl had received a note, brought by a negro who had instantly gallopped off into the woods.

There was company at the house, young ladies

with guitars, young fellows with gosling voices. She had declared that she had a headache, oh, so dreadful a headache, and had stolen away to wait and to listen. Why did he not come? Surely, he knew that she was there. His boat touched the garden; she was in his arms; they were sitting on the old brick wall.

"Oh, I thought you never would come," she said.

"But, precious, I am earlier than I have ever been before."

"Yes; but there are times when the very earliest minute is late—when sunrise is even late. Eve, when she first opened her eyes, could have said to Adam, 'Oh, how late you are!'"

He laughed at this conceit, and fondly kissed her. "You are such a bundle of thrills," he said.

"If you like thrills, I hope I am. I hope I'm anything you want me to be. But do you know that I have been thinking about that woman?"

"What woman, precious?"

"The hateful creature you said you once liked so well. I know she's a fright, and just as despicable as she can be, but men don't care for that. They can love a fright just as well as they can anybody. You've seen her since you saw me."

" No, little girl, I have not; but it would make no difference how often I might see her. I couldn't love her."

" But she must be smarter than I am. How can you, a great strong man, love me—when I am so weak? Mother is right—I am foolish. But I didn't know that I was going to love you so."

" Your mother is a strong-minded woman, precious, but she's wrong when she calls you foolish."

" How do you know she's strong-minded?"

" Because I am a pretty fair judge."

" But how can you judge her when you don't know her?"

" I do know her, little one. I told you that the governor was going to grant my pardon, didn't I? Well, he did. I heard in some mysterious way that your brother was to be taken to the mountains, and as I could go with him without danger, I decided to do so, and I did. I got on the train near the place where I met you, and I introduced myself as your brother's friend. I requested your mother not to mention me in any of her letters home, that I had slipped off for a brief rest and didn't want any one to know where I was."

" And you did all that for me? You are the kindest and noblest man in the world."

" No, but I am doing everything I can to re-deem myself. A reformed man may not be the best, but he is never the worst. And I believe that by devoting my life to you, I shall fitly atone for the evil I have done."

" Dear, you haven't done any evil. Of course, it wasn't exactly right to rob trains, but you gave back the money as nearly as you could. Old Jude, the colored man who works about here, says that it doesn't make any difference what you do just so you praise the Lord while you are doing it."

" A consoling idea," he replied, laughing; " but I don't think that one would feel disposed to sing a hymn while robbing a train. But, really, I never was vicious in my railroad work. And when I announced that I was done, the three men who had been my companions threatened to kill me."

" And what has become of them?" she eagerly asked, clutching his arm.

" They were hanged a few days ago in Arkan-sas."

" But didn't they try to implicate you?"

" Yes, but that made no difference, **for the governor had already signed my pardon.**"

She was silent, with her head on his boson..
They heard the soft thrum of a guitar and the
strained notes of a gosling voice.

Suddenly she lifted his head and sought to
look into his eyes. " You are not jealous, and
that proves what? That you can't love me very
much."

He laughed softly and pressed her head to his
bosom. " Jealousy is a matter of temperament
more than of love," he replied. " I have perfect faith in you."

" Then I'm glad you aren't jealous. But
really it would give me more confidence if you
were to be jealous just a little bit. It would at
least prove that you are anxious about me. But
if you ever love me any less, just the tiniest
speck, won't you tell me; won't you please ?"

" Precious, I could never love you any less.
Haven't you reformed me ? Haven't you made
a man of me ?"

" But I don't want you to love me simply because I reformed you."

" The reform came out of my love for you,"
he replied. " Now let us talk about our plans,"
he added. " The marriage, as I before remarked, must take place openly in the house.
Some of the strictest of the people hereabout

may be shocked at the idea of your giving your-self to an ex-robber, but we can't help that."

"It's none of their business," she replied. "Do they think I could love a clod-hopper? Oh, I hate commonplace people. The mere fact that a man is good doesn't commend him to me. Anybody can be good."

They sat there on the wall, listening to the guitar and the young man with the gosling voice. The stars must have come closer, for the garden grew lighter. A whipporwill, wandering from the distant hills, alighted on a sapling near the ruined summer house and sent his sad trill far across the quiet night.

"A whipporwill," she said, looking up. "Prob-ably he came from the mountains where my poor brother lies suffering. And here I have sat, selfishly thinking about myself and haven't asked you about him. Do you think he will get well? You do, don't you?"

"Surely. He is one of the strongest of men. It rests principally with the nursing, and you must know that a mother is always a good nurse. Who is at the house?"

"Some young people from the village."

"But won't they think that your absence is rather strange?"

" No, I am supposed to have gone to bed with a headache.   Rose can entertain them."

" Who is Rose ?"

" Haven't I told you about her ?   Surely I have been thinking about myself all the time.   She is a young lady who has been boarding with us for some time.   And I don't want you to see her, for you would surely fall in love with her."

" Has your brother seen her ?"

" Of course he has."

" Did he fall in love with her ?"

For a time she was silent.   " He is not like any one else," she said.   " He is so strong—but yes, I believe he is in love with her.   I know he is.   But will you promise not to fall in love with her?   What is the use, though, of making a promise ?   You couldn't keep it.   Now I know I am just as foolish as I can be.   I must stop it, mustn't I ?   Tell me, did you walk high in the air the night you first knew that I loved you?   I want to know if it affected you as it did me— were you in another world ?   Won't you please tell me ?"

" Little precious, that night I stubbed my toe on a star and fell over the moon."

" Oh, how sweet, how delicious.   I wish you would talk that way all the time.   But you have gone into business now, and I'm afraid that after a while you won't be as sentimental as you were when—when—"

" As when I was a traveling man?" he suggested, laughing at her, kissing her.

She laughed with him. She said it was charmingly funny, and then she was sad, doubting his love. But he told her that not within a thousand years could all his love flow through the channel of the Suwanee river—told her, again and again, that he had stubbed his toe on a star while looking up towards her. And his arms were about her. Words had lost their significance. Her faith was perfect and she cooed her happiness.

CHAPTER XVII.

The next day was the fifteenth **of the month,** but the minister's salary had not been sent to the house. On her way to the office Rose met the Mayor and he volunteered the information that the money had been forwarded to Mrs. Avery.

" Why, I thought it was to be sent to the house," she replied, nervously, for she saw that between her willingness and her ability to keep a promise a difficulty arose.

" Well, yes, that might have been expected, that is, of ordinary people, but we are more thoughtful, and therefore sent the money directly to the mountains where it will do the most good."

The Commodore appeared to be worried when Rose found him in his accustomed seat against the wall, and his brass anchor was dull. As she entered he took off his cap and threw it toward a table. It fell on the floor, and he let it lie there.

" Miss Rose," said he, " I am **split up the back like a locust.**"

" I am very sorry, Commodore."

" Ah, and if you are truly sorry, I have already found a compensating consolation. But I am sad, bowed down, and humiliation has slit my ears. Miss Rose, Sappho is going to marry Dr. Block."

" Oh, I am *so* sorry to hear that, Commodore. She is intelligent and refined, and how can she marry that coarse creature ?"

" Miss Rose, you have now been associated with me long enough to pardon my harmless but at the same time semi-profane promptings; so, therefore, I earnestly and fervently hope that you will grant me the privilege of saying this: It seems to me that a bright and refined woman is eternally on the look-out for some damned fool. There now, please pardon me, for I didn't know exactly how it would sound, and in reality be it truthfully said I didn't care."

" But do you really think she will marry him ? "

" Miss Rose, it is my nature to lead gently up to a disagreeable truth. Ah, do I really think so ? Miss Rose, they are already married—they were married last night; and when I left home this morning, he, my son-in-law, the husband of my cultured offspring,—he was out in the bot holding Sappho with one hand and a lame horse's hoof with the other. Yes, that was the status of the case when I left home. And when I looked back from the brow of the hill, he was kissing Sappho but had not turned loose the horse's hoof. Can an American father, a man who has distinguished himself fighting—fighting against his country—I ask can an American father be called upon to put up with more than that ? "

" I am sorry, Commodore," the girl said, striving to hide her mirth—" I am indeed more sorry than it would be prudent to express."

" Yes," replied the Commodore, " but it couldn't be helped, and we must therefore hope for the best. But to hope is to acknowledge a fear. Indeed, I might say that hope springs *infernal* in the human breast. What have I done all my life but hope ? Fate says, ' Why, good morning, Commodore. Delighted to see you. Wish I had more time to spare with you but I haven't. Remember this, however. When you can't do anything else you can hope.' "

" My regret is mixed with just a little selfishness," she said, after a short silence. " I am compelled to ask a favor of you to-day, and yet this infliction—"

"Miss Rose," he broke in, "don't hesitate to ask a favor of me. Remember that I am your most willing as well as most obedient servant. What can I do?"

"Now remember that I am compelled to ask it. Will you remember that?"

"Bird from the sunset—I mean, my dear friend—I will remember anything you may request me to charge my mind with. If you should say, 'Commodore, remember that you are dead,' the breath would gradually leave my body, and people meeting one another on the street would whisper, 'well, the old sea dog has gone at last.' Name the favor that I can confer upon you."

"Can you advance me twenty-five dollars? I have some money, but not enough for my purpose. Can you without inconvenience let me have that amount?"

"Miss Rose, your request, as light and trifling as it may be, thrills me with delight, and takes away much of the sting of seeing that fellow holding my daughter with one hand and a horse's hoof with the other. I have money lying idle, ready to be burned, in fact; and I will hasten this minute and get you the required sum."

He arose, and without stopping to stretch himself, as was his wont, caught up his cap and hastened to the office of a lawyer. "Judge," said he, bowing and giving his trousers a comic-opera hitch, "I have a very important transaction on hand. Lately I have disposed of large landed estates, but the fact is I have not as yet received full and satisfactory payment for the same, which, as you may readily conceive, being a man of most sensitive intuition, places me at a slight disadvantage in this rip-roaring commercial world. So now, if you will lend me twenty-five dollars I will pay you back so soon that you will really be astonished at the headlong speediness with which I can transact a piece of business."

"Adams, I don't believe I have that amount of money to spare," the lawyer replied.

"Judge, in my humility, brought about by a mere trick of commerce, I will pardon the omission of my title, but I entreat you not to be unnecessarily harsh. I will sign any sort of paper that your skillful brain may devise, but please don't be so sternly impetuous as to say that you can't let me have the money. Now, I am worth about as much as any man in this town. You know that. But the trouble is I am short of ready cash, and when a man is in that condition he feels that fate is flogging him with cat o' nine tails, made out of his own heart-strings."

" Adams, on one condition I will let you have the money."

" Most generous and upright jurist, hand over the money and name your condition at your earliest convenience or at your dignified leisure."

" The condition always first, Adams."

" Commodore."

" Condition always first, Adams.   And this is the condition: You must return the money to-morrow.   It belongs to a client."

" Who is he, Judge?"

" Old man Holloway."

" What!   Judge, yc .. delight me.   Old man Holloway is one of my most fervent admirers, and I will give you the money to-morrow even if I have to borrow it from him.   Judge, I thank you, I thank you most profoundly, sir."

When he returned to the office, Rose said she hoped that to advance the money had put him to no trouble.   " Miss Rose," he replied, feeling for his brass anchor, " if a pleasure is a trouble, then indeed am I inflicted.   Bless your heart, the money was idle, actually moulding, and it was my duty to stir it up.   Hush, here comes the happy couple."

Dr. Block and his wife came in, bowing and smiling.   " We don't want any congratulations," said Sappho. " and especially do we protest against commonplaces."

" Not a com.," the " doctor " agreed, tapping his head.

" Miss Rose," Sappho went on, after giving the doctor an approving smile, " you needn't tell us that you are glad or sorry. We were old enough to please ourselves and we have done so. The doctor may not be a society man, but he is the dearest character on earth."

" Tap, tap," came from the doctor's head.

" And we don't need any sympathy," Sappho continued. " Don't need the lukewarm water of commiseration, and won't have it. So that point is settled. I expect to travel about the country with the doctor, and then I may have an opportunity to display what talent I possess. I have learned that after all it is contact that makes us wise. Eh, doctor?"

" Tap, tap."

" Yes, contact with other minds. I was wasting myself here. But I don't think that father is at all pleased with the doctor, which argues that he does not appreciate the sublime, not in art but in oddity."

" Wait," said the Commodore, wiping his face with a red handkerchief. " I appreciate the doctor's good points and therefore be it said that we will not clash. I admit that I expected you to look higher, but I am willing to agree that you know best. Doctor, treat her with the tenderest kindness, sir, or I shall draw off more of your blood than you can well spare."

" She's a thoroughbred and will get the best treatment," the doctor replied. " I know how to treat a thoroughbred."

" All right, sir. But take her away now, as we have on hand a business matter—"

" Oh, father, how can you at a time like this ? " Sappho cried.

The Commodore looked steadily at her and was silent, but the working of his countenance, the rising and falling of his fierce eye-brows, told that he was thinking; and the product of his mental activity was not long under cover. " My daughter, there was a time when that sort of a protest had a certain charm. There was in it a languid and not unmusical plea—it was a hot-house plant shrinking from a crack in the glass when a sliver of cold air is driven in, but that time is over. A woman who—and I say this without prejudice—I affirm that a woman who can marry a horse-doctor, one who holds her with one hand and the split hoof of a horse with the

other, can put up with most anything.   Go on
now and give your friends throughout the village
a chance to congratulate you.   No harm done.
Run along."

At evening a rain swept up the river, but when
midnight came down out of the black clouds and
lay upon the land, Rose stood at the bottom of
the garden, waiting for a boat.   It came.   A
voice cried " I am here " and she replied, " So
am I."

" But who are you?" the boatman asked,
climbing the slippery bank.

" I am Mr. Avery's sister.   He could not come.
Here is your money."

" Thanks.   You don't know what it's for, do
you?"

" I don't know and I don't care.   Take it and
go."

" Thanks."

She heard him " slopping" down the slippery
bank, heard the dipping of his oars mingled with
the dash of the rain.

Upon returning to the house she was scolded
by Ellen.   " Why, where on earth have you
been at this time of night, and out in this awful
rain, too?   What made you slip off from me?
You mustn't do me that way when I think so much

of you. But I ought not to scold to-night. We have received some good news. The mail was late, but the postmaster has just sent out a letter from mother. Brother Louis is getting well."

CHAPTER XVIII.

The cool air of the mountain had blown
Avery's fever back to the cypress swamps, far below the village of Gaeta. "He is getting stronger
every minute," Mrs. Avery wrote, "and it does
me good to hear him ask for something to eat.
Yesterday he had an argument with a Methodist
preacher, but he departed somewhat from the
faith, and this grieved me, more and more as I realized that all my dependence in this life rests upon
his faithfulness to the church of his fathers. Immediately upon coming here I wrote to my brother
and I have just received some money from him, and
I don't think that anything ever came at a better
time, for my son will not come back when I do,
but will travel about the country for a short time
to get back his strength and spirits. I wish you
would thank the deacon for sending my son's
salary. I haven't mentioned it, for as my son
announced his intention not long ago of practic-
ing the most rigid economy, the close judgment
exercised by the Pilgrim Fathers, I did not want
him to know that we were practically without a

reserve at home. I will keep the money untouched and bring it home with me. I may return the latter part of the week, and then, my daughter, I shall tell you of a gentleman who met us at the railway. He came all the way up here with us and seemed to be perfectly devoted to your brother. But the strangest part of it is this: When he was gone and when Louis had a brief return of reason, I told him about his friend and he didn't know anything about him. It is all very singular, I am sure."

Rose read the letter, then went to her room and sat down alone. The references to Avery sounded so far off. They were like the echo of words heard in a dream. If he were growing stronger, why did he not write to her? Was his love for her a fever and had the mountain air blown it away? She wondered whether he had ever loved any one She knew that women must have loved him. One by one she pictured every feature of his face—his strong, clear eyes, his refined mouth, and she could hear his voice in the rain pattering on the leaves of the vine at the window.

The next morning she was not well enough to go to the office, and Ellen was sent to tell the Commodore. The blockade-runner was already in his accustomed place when the girl entered the room. " Why, bless my life, come in," he cried, rubbing his eyes and staring at her. " You and Miss Rose are so much alike that I can scarcely tell you apart. Didn't she come with you?"

" No, sir; and I have come to tell you that she isn't well enough to come to-day."

" Why, I'm mighty sorry to hear that. Hope she isn't very sick. Some people ought to be sick and some oughtn't—some ought to be dead, in fact—but she ought never to have a pain. About how sick do you think she is?"

" Only a headache. Won't you let me do her work?"

The Commodore put on his cap, touched the anchor, and thus replied: " My dear young lady, nothing would give me more pleasure than to see you sit at that desk, and I urge you to sit there, but it would require many years of practice to enable you to do that woman's work. Miss Ellen, law may be complicated and theology may be a hotbed of dispute, but the real estate business is a boiling whirlpool. And but few people have ever mastered its seething details. Man's first trouble was to lose his title to a garden. No, you can only inspire me, that's all. By the way, did you hear of my daughter's marriage?"

" Yes, sir, and I am sorry; that is, if you want me to be."

" Hah, delicately said. I am getting over my soreness—with the aid of will-force and Christian fortitude, I have tempered the ice bath into which I was plunged, therefore be it said, I don't now want you to be as sorry as I would have wanted you to be yesterday. But I confess that in my ears can still be seen the slits of humiliation. How was your noble brother when you last heard from him ? "

" Nearly well, and we look for mother soon. She is coming home alone, for brother is going to travel for a short while."

" Best thing he could do. But he ought to go to salt water. Land travel is an abomination in the sight of Him who walked on the sea. We must sail—we must run a blockade now and then. But, really, I don't think he ought to stay away very long. We need him. When he goes away our church bleeds, but there is another cause why he should hasten back. On this earth, Miss Ellen, the strongest of all claims is the sentimental claim; therefore, be it said, that if any one should have a sentimental claim on you, don't stay away from him any longer than you can help. I don't presume to say that any one

has a sentimental claim on you, understand; but,
if some one has—"

"Some one has, Commodore."

"Ha, that so? Now, you know that I am
sorry? Pardon me, but I thought that if no one
had that sort of a claim, I would like—now, not
to be abrupt, but at the same time to preserve
the correct forms of business—I would like to
submit a bid. But we will not open that bid, if
another one has been accepted. Yes, delightful
to know that some one has a sentimental sight
draft against you—a judgment note of the heart.
Well, run along now—I mean don't stay away
from him any longer than you can help. I know
what sentiment is, Miss Ellen. We, sentiment
and I, have played together, hand in hand, and
we have wept together, cheek to cheek, which
therefore be it said, means tear for tear. But
along came business with its shaggy hair and
imperious growl, its gnarled horns, and I had—I
had to kiss sentiment a sorrowful good-bye.
Hah, and when you go home you may tell Miss
Rose that we can not permit her the luxury of a
long illness, for I am threatened with a rush of
business. I feel it in the air and I know it's
coming. Therefore tell her to brace herself
against any advance of her indisposition. Ah

but tell her also not to come back too soon; impress her with the fact that I am strong and can push hard against a coming struggle. Must you go now? I am deeply sorry. Inspired by your presence I could knock a worry on the head and kill it. When your mother comes, give her my thrice warmed regards and don't forget to assure her that I missed her greatly during her absence."

CHAPTER XIX.

Rose remained in her room until after the noon hour and then she came out to walk in the garden. A flight of swallows whirled up the river, like streaks of night in the glowing air of the fervid day, and the hen that had led her chickens to play in the cool dust under the snow ball bushes, croaked a distressful warning to her brood.

On the broken wall the girl sat, watching old Jude cast his throw line. From his canoe he saw her, and slowly shaking his head he cried:

"Feesh gittin' so purtickler deze days da doan wanter eat whuts sot befo' 'em. Yas, sah—I means yassum—da's gittin' ter put on a'rs an' doan wanter bite lessen er pusson puts on er little style hiss'f. But I tell you de fust ting da knows da'll be glad er nuff ter git er hunk o' fat meat. Folks ain' gwine ter humor 'em allus—ain' gwine ter put up wid 'em, I tell you. Did you see dat bright raskil jump up dar an' meck er mouf at me? But neber mine. Git him atter w'ile, an' w'en I gits him I gits him good."

" Uncle Jude can you get a boat light enough for me to pull ? I want to go down the river."

" I don't know'm 'bout gittin' er boat light er nuff fur dem putty arms ter pull. Better let me take you whar you wan' ter go, ma'am."

" No, I want to go alone."

" All right, ma'm, you kin take dis yere cunner an' I kin git de boat. Dat'll feex it. Come right down yere an' git in. Yere I come an' yere I is."

In the canoe she lightly paddled down the stream. She was nervous and feverish, but the cool air coming up from the gulf refreshed her; and mingled with the suggested sniff of salt water, came the sweet, fresh scent of the nameless flowers that bloomed in the marsh. She appeared to be making for some special place, for critically she gazed at the banks and the trees, and finally she turned the canoe toward the shore and stepped upon the sand under a live-oak that leaned far over the water. Now she was certain of her bearings, and through the woods she walked, sometimes with rapid strides and then with slower steps, as if keeping pace with a varying mood. After going some dis-tance she looked about her, and then hastening to a log, sat down upon it and reverentially turned her eyes toward the vine cross. She felt Avery's spiritual presence, but she could not feel that he loved her. If he did love her, how could he treat her with such indifference? Suddenly she sprang up, ran to a weed, plucked its purple top, and pinned the bloom on her bosom. Then she sat down again to think. She wondered why Avery had chosen her to give the man fifty dollars. Why did not the fellow come to the house if money were due him? Why did he come in the dark? Off in the deep shade her fancy sketched the preacher's countenance. She gazed at it, saw it rise and fall; and just as she thought that it was fading, shrinking further back amid the deeper shadows, it flew to her, and vivid, hung before her eyes. The expression of the face was, as she had so often seen it, troubled and sad; the eyes tender but deeply serious, with a melancholy reproach. But in that countenance she could find no expression of love. And then her pride sprang up and the face vanished. She condemned herself. How could he love her when she had made no concealment of her love for him? A man must feel a contempt for the woman who throws her love at him. From her bosom she tore the flower and threw it away. And when she turned toward the canoe, her mind had seized a resolve and desperately was hugging it. She would leave Gaeta.

She found it almost impossible to paddle against the current, and even by pursuing the still water wind ags along the shore her progress was slow. She heard some one rowing, and looking back saw a man in a skiff, pulling as if it were his aim to overtake her. He was not far off, and a few more strokes brought him within talking distance.

" I'll hitch to and tow you up," he said turning his skiff toward her.

" No, thank you. I can get along well enough."

But he came alongside, caught up the chain at the end of the canoe, fastened it to the stern of the skiff, and regardless of her protests pulled out into deeper water. He sat facing her, gazed at her and he was a loathsome creature.

" Has your brother got back ?" he asked.

" Sir ?"

" Has your brother got back? I reckon not though. Heard that they had hauled him to the mountains."

She looked at him, his yellow countenance, his insulting grin " He has not returned," she said.

" Gettin' better, ain't he ?"

" Yes."

" Any idee when he will be back ?"

" No."

" Don't know me, do you ?   Didn't see me, or rather talk to me last night, I reckon ?"

" Will you please unfasten that chain ?"

" Oh, I ain't tired yet."

" But I *am*.   Unfasten that chain."

" Yes, when we git up here a little further.   I always like to help a person along—natural with me—and I notice that we generally do the most good when we help the person that don't want to be helped.   Think a good deal of your brother, I reckon.   Great man—ain't no doubt about that.   Game, and that makes him mighty nigh all right in this part of the country. · But are you right certain he's your brother ?"

" I demand of you to unfasten that chain."

" Oh, we're getting along all right."

" Yes," she replied, with seeming resignation, " and really I am grateful for your kindness; and when my brother returns I shall request him to thank you."

The fellow ceased rowing.   The boats drifted. " Then you do know me, don't you ?   Of course, if you insist I'll cut loose, but I don't see why you should object to letting me haul you up. To tell you the truth, I ain't right at myself on the present occasion. Met a feller down yonder and he invited me to tilt a swamp jug and I tilted her once too often. I'll take you over to the still water and drop you."

He took up his oars and headed his skiff toward the garden shore. " Hope you won't tell your brother that I worried you any. If you tell him anything at all you might sorter hint that you met me and incidentally found out that I was so hard pressed for money that I'll have to have a double allowance next time. That will be about the right sort of caper to cut. Well, I'll drop you here and beg your pardon."

Sadly she walked through the garden toward the house, turning from one dimly traced pathway into another, avoiding a straight course, loth to leave this tangled bough-work, the woven briars and bushes. Here her heart had been caught, and here she knew that forever it must remain. But she would go away; her pride, now seeming long to have been dormant, had arisen to make a merciless demand of her and she must obey. Under a fig tree near the ruins of the old summer house she paused, for it was here that Avery's spiritual presence was strongest, and here she stood, not looking about her, but with her eyes closed. It would be cruel to leave Eller alone, but in pride's demand there is always a semblance of justice, and justice can strike no compromise, can take no account of cruelty.

She went to her room and was packing her trunk when Ellen came singing up the stairway; and hastily Rose put away all evidences of her intention to leave. She must go away as she had come, by stealth. Radiant with careless happiness, Elen entered the room. " Why, you are as smart as you can be," she said. " Just get well whenever you want to, don't you. And won't you please pardon me for staying away so long? But I really couldn't help it. After I left the Commodore, and I had to stay there quite a while, I was compelled to go to the dressmaker's, and you know what that means. Gracious, it's warm! And you look as if you had been out in the sun. But it makes no difference how warm it is, I've got to go back. Of course there weren't goods enough. And I ought to have attended to it at once, but I had to come and see you. Do you care if I go back now?"

" Surely not. You must go."

" But if you don't want me to I won't."

" I want you to go."

"I knew you would, you are such a dear. I'll be back as soon as I can."

She ran down the stairs, laughing; and tearfully Rose resumed her packing. The evening breeze grew stronger, blowing straight up the river, and the vine at the window hoarsely whispered. Her work was done, and now it was her intention to request Jude to take her to the railway station. But she must leave some word, some sign of regret, of affection, and she sat down to write a note to Elen, but all she left upon the writing desk, when she went out, was a piece of blank paper, tear-stained. Once more she went to the garden, and this time she did not pause under the fig tree, but she gathered a bouquet of roses and straightway ran to Avery's study. She put the flowers on his dresser and stood looking at them. Night was coming; lonesome noises, faint, reminiscent, were heard afar off in the woods. A bat flew in at the window. She heard Jude calling the cows. She ran to her room, threw herself upon the bed, sobbed herself to sleep; and when she awoke a new sun was shining and her resolve to go away was dead.

CHAPTER XX.

Avery went with his mother to the train one morning, and when homeward bound she was gone, he turned his own face toward Denver. He had not told his mother whither he was going. He spoke of several cities, but studiedly suppressed the name of the Colorado metropolis. To the hotel had come a mind reader, and in the parlor at night, with the shrewd art of his profession he mystified the guests; and in his presence Avery was afraid to think of the influence that was drawing him toward Denver.

"I don't care to talk to you on the subject of your intellectual magic," he said to the man when invited to explore the mystery of a test. "I have no faith in such trickery."

"But if I should take hold of your hand and tell your thoughts, you would—"

"Don't touch me, sir. I will give no countenance to any sort of jugglery."

Avery bought his railway ticket, not through to Denver, but to a small city in Illinois. The agent remarked that he could sell a stop-over ticket for that point, and Avery, giving him a hard look, replied :

"How do you know, sir, that I desire to go any further? What right have you to pre-sume —"

"I beg your pardon, sir."

He felt that the fever had left his mind clearer than it had been during the few weeks preceding the disease. A sermon came to him almost at a bound, and bits of Greek verse, long ago forgot-ten, flew twittering out of the dark, and like birds, perched upon his memory, sang to him; and yet he realized that on one subject his mind was sadly morbid. He reasoned with himself, and his reasoning was sharp, but the edge trimmed off no difficulties. And at night, on the sleeping car, when the train roared around the rough curves of a jagged country, he lay looking back into his soul, searching for the cross and the crucified Galilean. But he found no cross, no Galilean, saw only the sad and appealing eyes of a beautiful woman. He heard some one talking to the porter. "What's the name of this car?"

"The Denver, sah," the porter answered.

He had thought to change his mind, to pass the Illinois town, but arriving at that place, he left the train, checked his trunk at the station, and went wandering about the streets. Another train was due at midnight, and before ten o'clock he returned to the station and sat down to wait. What purpose had he served by getting off? He called himself a fool.

" This thing of waiting for a train is a pretty tiresome thing," an old man said to him.

" Yes."

" I got here this morning, and have been here ever since. Dropped off to sleep, and they let me miss one train. They ought to be taught to understand their business better than that. I thought they had to wake people up, but it seems that they don't. How far are you going?"

" A long distance."

" So am I. I haven't taken a long trip since I came from the East when I was a boy, and this journey sorter makes me open my eyes. I've been living near here all by myself for some time but my son wants me to come to him. Lives out in Denver and I'm going there. Happen to be going as far as that?"

" Yes."

" Live out that way, I reckon?"

" No."

" Where is your home?"

" I can scarcely call any place home."

" That so? Well, you know the oid saying has it that it's home where the heart is."

" Yes, and that's the reasou I can scarcely place my home."

" That so? Well, I know pretty much how you feel. Been all along there. I've fit against hot winds and army worms and grasshoppers in my time till I'll be dinged if it appeared that there was such a thing as a home anywhere."

Again he was on the train roaring toward Denver; and mountains arose into view at morning. He grew more nervous as the day advanced, as the mountains became clearer cut in the distance, and when at last he left the train in Denver, he stood about dazed, scarcely knowing which way to turn. But he drove to a hotel, registered and walked about the streets. Now what was he to do? What had he come for? To learn the truth. But how was he to learn it? By walking about the streets? It was growing late, for the theaters were out when he went into a café. He sat down, ordered a cup of coffee, and as he sat there, waiting, out of the clatter of dishes and the rasping noises of chairs grating on the mosaic floor, came the words of two men who sat near him.

"I never did know the particulars," said one of the men, "but I understand that she killed him instantly."

Avery went out. Was that tragedy still so fresh in the public mind? But if he wanted to learn, why had he run away? He returned to the hotel, went to bed and lay awake until nearly daylight, shrewdly planning. He agreed with his judgment that he must get every detail of Powell's death, every leading, every drift; but upon himself he must put the force of such mastery as would blunt the appearance of keen concern. He would go to the office of a daily newspaper and search the files. He went, and after finding the startling head-lines, gazed at them until the black words ran into one another and meant nothing. Slily, when no one was looking, he cut out the "report" and stuffed it into his pocket. He knew that this was abusing a confidence, and he condemned himself, but in his desperation he reasoned that it was necessary. In his room he smoothed out the paper and strove to read the words. Rose Grayham was the girl's name. She was beautiful; was of an old Virginia family. Her father, a striking type of the American gentleman, had invested largely in mining interests, had died suddenly and had left little or no available property.   The girl was popular, was said to possess great musical gifts, and with some little assistance had fought her way to Wellesly and had returned not with a determination to pursue the study of music but with a passion for art.

Avery could but catch a sentence here and there, and he tore the paper into bits.   But he had seized the name of the fashionable boarding house wherein the man had been killed, and thither he went the next morning.   He did not send in his name, but asked to see the owner of the place.   A dignified woman came out into the hall.   "Madam," said he, "I shall be in the city a short time, and as I dislike the noise of a hotel, I should like to stay in your house."

"I shall be pleased to entertain you, sir.   It is my custom to demand a reference, but I suppose I may dispense with that in your case." She gave him the trained smile of society, that skillful lighting of the countenance which, beaming upon even an awkward man, puts him at ease; and courteously she added: "Please step into the drawing room."

He entered a large room dark with rich furniture, and the first thing that his eye rested upon was a piano. He took a seat and the woman stood near him, pleasantly talking.

" So, you don't know, then, how long you may remain ?"

" No, madam; but only a short time."

" Of course you have been here quite often ? "

" No, this is my first visit."

" Indeed ! Then you must find much to interest you ?"

" Yes, it is a charming city. You have lived here a long time, I presume?"

" Yes, nearly all my life. I have seen the city grow from nothing."

" Won't you please sit down ?" he asked.

" I really haven't time, but I will, just for a few moments."

" Thank you," he said; and after a silence, after looking afar off through a window, he remarked, " The life of Denver has been an enthusiasm and a tragedy, and I suppose you have seen all its moods?"

" Yes, indeed. A part of its tragedy was enacted in this room."

" Indeed ! "

" Yes, a man named Powell was killed right over there at the piano."

" A murder ? "

" Well, that was what the newspapers called it, but I think that it must have been justifiable.

He was killed by Rose Grayham, the most beautiful woman I ever saw, the gentlest and most
lovable person, but withal a peculiar girl,
whimsical and morbidly sensitive. I often think
about her, for she impressed me deeply. At
morning I have seen her so joyous that she was
almost hysterical, at noon she would be serious
with the strongest common sense, and at evening she would wish that she were dead. We
never could find out all about the killing. Miss
Georgia Morton saw the shot fired, saw Powell
fall, and she told all that she knew, of course,
but we never could get at the cause—we could
only surmise that it must have been a love quarrel."

" Then there is no doubt as to the fact that
she killed him ?"

" Oh, none whatever."

" What sort of looking man was Powell ?"

" Tall, with light hair. He would have re-
sembled you had his hair and eyes been darker.
But will you please excuse me a moment ?"

" Just one word more. Miss Grayham lived in
this house ?"

" Yes, and I knew her intimately, of course.
Everybody loved her. Why, the night before the
tragedy she sang in the opera house, at a charit-

able entertainment, and the audience went almost wild with enthusiasm."

" Wait just one more moment. You will please pardon my not introducing myself. I am a minister of the gospel, not a saintly man, but one with many weaknesses."

" And your name ?"

" I am going to remain so short a time that my name can be of no moment."

" Oh, have you come to take a part in the Sam Jones meetings ? They have built a great tabernacle for him, and the town is wild with religious excitement."

" I may possibly render some assistance before I leave, but I did not come with that purpose in view. Madam, I am very much interested in the story you have told me. I might say that Miss Grayham and I were friends, long ago, in Virginia. I do not affirm this, but I might say it— might declare that her father was my friend."

She gave him a searching look. " Are you sure that you are not a detective ?" she asked.

" Madam, I am sure that I am a preacher, and that the interest I take in that young woman has nothing to do with what the law might call justice. To tell you the truth, I would shield her from the law."

She was standing now, and keeenly she searched his face. " And you don't care to tell me your name?"

" I really don't see why I should not. My name is Avery, and I have a church in the far South."

" And you know where Rose Grayham is?"

" I didn't say so."

" But I see that you do. And won't you please tell me? I won't breathe it to a living soul."

" I can tell you nothing, and I request you not to mention what I have already been indiscreet enough to say. I don't know why I said so much. It was far from my intention, and is now condemned by my judgment."

" I would like to know more, but if you won't tell me, and I see that you will not, you may at least depend upon my saying nothing about what you have said."

" Madam, I thank you. Would you permit me to see the room in which she slept?

" Yes, I will show you up just as soon as I come back."

She went out, gracefully bowing, and Avery opened the piano, expecting to find blood on the keys. Was that a spot oi blood? Surely. He touched it—a speck of red lint.

The woman returned just as Avery resumed his seat. " If you will kindly walk up now I will show you the room," she said.

He followed her to a large, bright room on the second floor. " You can see how her mind was inclined," she said, pointing to the fanciful decorations on the wall.   Avery gazed about him, at a bold sketch of an old water-mill, and at the illustration of a poem, a spinning girl, binding with a strand of her hair the wounded leg of a stork shot by the prince in his playful humor.

" Madam, I should like to occupy this room."

" Yes, but you see there is no bed.   I had it taken out immediately after Miss Grayham ran away—left us, I mean.   I can give you just as comfortable a room on this floor."

" Thank you.   And you say that a Miss Morton saw the killing ? "

" Yes, sir, Miss Georgia Morton."

" Where is she now ?"

" She lives here in the city."

" I should like to talk to her."

" I don't think that she would talk about the tragedy, sir.   In fact, I know she wouldn't.   She has refused many a time.   Come this way, please, and I will show you your room."

That night Avery tossed about on his bed.

There was no need of further investigation—it was all true. And now he could go home, pitying her but not loving her. His love was dead. It had suffered and had died slowly, of exhaustion. He got up, walked about the room, put on his clothes, went out into the corridor, stopped at a door and tried the knob. The door was locked. He took from his pocket a bunch of keys—and the key of his little white church, away down on the Suwanee River, turned back the bolt. He stepped inside and lighted the gas, and upon the floor he sat, gazing at the spinning girl binding up the wounded leg of the stork. Yes, his love was dead, not a gasp was left. The hours passed; there was no noise in the streets, not a sound within the house—yes, a sob. Upon his breast he lay and when morning came his eyes were red with weeping, with the tears that fell upon his dead heart.

CHAPTER XXI.

At an early hour Avery went out to the cemetery to look at Powell's grave. The sexton conducted him to a sodded mound, and upon it were pots of flowers.

" Who pays so much attention to this grave?" Avery asked.

" A young woman, sir," the sexton answered.

" What is her name?"

" Miss Morton, I think, sir."

" Did you know the man?"

" Not very well, but I knew him by sight— saw him walking along here only a few days before he was killed."

" Was he alone?"

" No, sir, two ladies were with him, and one of them was Miss Morton."

" And the other one?"

" The lady that they say killed him, sir."

Avery stood looking at the grave. His brow was moist but his eyes were dry. " This man came from the East, didn't he?"

" I heard them say that he did."

" Did you ever hear anyone say that he went under an assumed name ? "

" It seems to me that I heard something of the sort, but I didn't happen to pay much attention."

" What sort of a looking man was he ? "

" About your size, only not quite so tall."

Back toward the city the preacher strolled. He had stood at the grave of his brother and had not shed a tear; and for this he strove to reproach himself but could not feel his own censure, for his heart was dead.   As he walked along he was surprised at the degree of interest that he felt in ordinary things, a sprinkling cart, a horse grazing by the roadside, a dog scratching himself; and this pleased him, for it bespoke a healthy state of mind.   The mind could exist and be observing even if the heart were dead.   " The world's greatest men are heartless," he argued.   " A man to be great in the esteem of the public must be cold—he must constantly keep his mind on himself, must sacrifice friends, smother emotion—he must kill his heart."

He debated whether or not to call on Miss Morton.   But why should he see her ?   He could not hope to find a flaw in the proof.   And why should he hope to find a flaw ?   Rose Grayham was surely nothing to him.   He was sorry for her, but that was all.

At the boarding-house he sat alone in the parlor. Again he opened the piano and examined the keys. There was no stain anywhere, no blotch on the floor. But, of course, they had put down another carpet. He walked out into the hall, peeped about to see if any one might be looking, stole up the stairs, unlocked a door and stood gazing at a spinning girl and the stork. He entered, shut the door, locked it, and sat down with his back against the wall. He had not supposed that with so little of emotion he could look upon that sketch. And her graceful hand had swept those lines upon the wall. Her hand, not the hand he had held when he led her home up the river, but the hand that had slain his brother.

Evening came, and he went to the tabernacle wherein a great crowd was gathering. He sought the evangelist and thus spoke to him:

" I am a preacher—I have looked into my soul and have seen a Christ on a cross. And my love for that Christ has been strong and passionate. I could not look at Him calmly; it was almost with an agony of devotion. I have a favor to ask. It matters not what my name may be; I want no introduction, but to-night when you are done with your work, when you have urged sinners to come forward and put their galling burdens upon the altar. let me say a few words to these people."

The evangelist took him by the hand and witn these words replied, " We have need **not** of studied words but of utterances that break through the mouth.   You must talk."

The time came and Avery arose.   Hundreds had knelt to be prayed for and the harvest of re- pentence must all have been gathered; he could but be a gleaner.   His words came like a flight of martins at dusk; people gazed in astonishment at him, and when he sat down, a woman sprang to her feet and with her hands high in the air, ran forward and dropped upon her knees.

The services were done, the crowd was dispers- ing, and Avery was out in the street.   A number of people had sought to detain him, to shake hands with him, to compliment him, but he had pulled away from them.   Straightway he hastened to the railway station, and upon arriving there he remembered that he had left his trunk.   He drove back, urging the hackman to make all possible haste, but when he returned the train was gone. And now his only prospect was to wait until mid- night, and he waited, slowly walking up and down the platform.

At morning when he looked back at the moun- tains, he said: " My heart died there and left me free.   Yes, I have nothing now to chain me, but what have I to inspire me? What can I hold as an ambition? Can I preach the gospel of love, the brotherhood of man? If I don't feel love how can I preach it? At least I can do my duty. So can any disappointed man. There must be a titter in hell when at last a man, sore and crushed, resolves to do his duty."

He reached Gaeta at night. In a plantation wagon he was driven from the station to the village. The train was late and the hack had not waited.

Through the garden he picked his way to the ruins of the old summer house, and there he stood, looking about him. In Rose's room a light was burning, and he gazed at it, but he felt no emotion, only a cool and pitying sense of freedom. Out of the garden he passed, and walked rapidly down the river to the place where he had met her, and then he turned reluctantly and slowly walked back. Still he felt no emotion, and surely this was a strong test. He stood on the spot where he had fainted the day when the fever had mastered him, and now the lights were all out and Rose's room was dark. Nowhere was there a gleam of light, no moon, no stars—all was black and the heart of the world was dead. Again he picked his way to the old summer house, and on the damp mould he sat, waiting for the sun. A wave of gray came down the river. The birds began to flutter—daylight, and a dull and troubled sun struggled in the murky east. He heard the opening of a door, heard his mother calling the old negro. Quickly he strode toward her, and she, after standing for a moment in astonishment, looking, wondering, ran to him with a cry of joy.

"Oh, my son, thank God you are with me again!"

"Don't make any noise, mother. Come up to my room."

On the dresser was a vase of flowers. "She has put them there fresh every day," said Mrs. Avery, looking at him as he stood gazing at the roses. "But do please sit down and tell me about yourself. You look so much better. And where did you go? You couldn't have gone to many places, for you are here so soon. But it was a long time to me, my son."

He sat upon the bed-side, still gazing at the roses. "I soon grew tired of traveling and thought that I would better come home," he said. "And has she put fresh flowers there every day?"

"Yes, Ellen says every day while we were in the mountains. Louis, she is the noblest woman

I ever knew. But before I forget it—so you won't be worried about money matters—let me tell you that I have your entire salary for the —"

" What !" he exclaimed, springing to his feet and turning almost angrily upon her.

" Why, I have your salary untouched. The deacon forwarded it to me. Louis, what on earth is the matter with you ?"

" Why in the name of God didn't you tell me!" he cried.

" Because I thought I would make a pleasant surprise of it."

" But you have made a misery of it."

" Oh, I am so sorry if I have, but it seems that I never know what to do. How have I done wrong? What harm was there in keeping the money for you ? We haven't denied ourselves anything, I'm sure; so please don't be worried."

" Mother, I must see Rose at once."

" But you can't see her now, my son."

" I *will* see her. Go tell her to meet me in the parlor as soon as she can."

" But I don't understand. Won't you please explain ?"

" Not now. Go at once, please. If you don't—"

" Oh, I'll go, only I'd like to understand."

He hastened to the parlor. The day was now well advanced, and the room was yellow with light. He knew not what to think, how to think. All his plans had gone wrong. He heard some- one coming down the stairs, but the foot-steps did not thrill him. Rose stepped into the room, and his heart leaped up from the dead, and with a sob he caught his breath. He turned away from her—he stood trembling in a strange fright, the fright of his heart's resurrection.

" Oh, Mr. Louis !"

He turned toward her, and oh, the beautiful innocence of her face, the glory of her eyes!

" I am so glad to see you, Mr. Louis."

" I thank you. Yes, I am feeling very well, only the trip has agitated me. I have some- thing to say to you—I have just received a great shock—yes, your hand, the other one. Mother tells me that my salary was forwarded to her. And you know I expected you to take fifty dollars of it—but you couldn't. The man in the garden at night—"

" I met him, Mr. Louis, and gave him the money."

" Oh, you—but where did you get the money —I mean did you give it to him ?"

" Yes, I had twenty-five dollars an' the Com- modore advanced twenty-five more."

" It must be paid back at once.

" No, not now, Mr. Louis.   Don't let it worry you, please, when it was such a pleasure to me."

" But it was wrong.   I'm going out—I want to be alone.   I'll see you—see you again."

Across the garden he strode, treading down the bushes, bending the saplings; and the briars caught him and strove to hold him but he tore himself loose from them.   He leaped so hard into a boat that he almost upset it, and grab-bing the oars, shoved off and sped away on the current.   Where the trees were thick he landed; through the woods he hastened; on a log he sat gazing at the vine cross.   "Unless I get some sort of relief I know that I shall go mad," he cried. " Why was I influenced to believe that my heart was dead ?   Why should I be constantly deceived ? Is it because I can not look into my heart and see the Man on the cross ? But did I take Him away? Oh, with my clearer vision, with my discernment strengthened by so much proof, I thought that upon her face I should surely find the marks of guilt, but they were not there.   Guilt! What sort of guilt ?   Revenge, impulsive justice.   And if with justice on her side she slew my brother, why should I condemn her ? She had a right, al-most a divine right, to kill him.   But great God,

she had no right to let him wrong her.   One was
a crime against the law, the other an outrage
against the soul—my soul.   And her love can
never more be strong and pure.   But I will forgive her.   Poor child, I pity her, but can I
marry her?   I will give her my sympathy, will be
careful not to wound her, but I can not tell her
of my love.   So now, with resignation and ten-
derness in the heart that I thought was dead, I
can go to her.   And to-morrow I will meet my
people at church and again play the hypocrite.
But how is it all to end?   I can not foresee; I
will simply look from one minute to the next and
not beyond.   I know that there must be an end
near, but I don't want to see it.   Yes, I must be
gentle with her, for she is in want of sympathy.
I have been brutal.   I will be a man."

Slowly he rowed up the river, growing stronger
and gentler as he advanced.   But he was not yet
the master of himself, for the oars fell from his
hands when he reached the place where the girl
had poured water on her head.   The boat drifted.
But his strength returned with a throb and he
caught up the oars and pulled steadily until the
landing was reached.   Ellen was at the bottom of
the garden, waiting for him.   She ran to him,
trying to talk, but she could only twitter with happiness.   She fondly kissed him.

" Has mother told you that I am soon to be married ? " she asked, leading him up the bank.

" No, little girl, she hasn't mentioned it."

" Well, that's cool, I'm sure. Is it so very light as all that ? Come over here and I'll tell you all about it. But will you promise me not to scold ?"

" Yes; I promise anything.'

" Oh, but you mustn't say that. When we promise anything we break all our promises; and we are not interested when we agree to promise anything. Now sit down here and I'll tell you all about it. But you mustn't laugh. Will you promise not to laugh ? Don't say you'll promise anything, but just promise not to laugh, and then scold me. Will you ?"

" Yes, go ahead."

" Oh, but you mustn't say ' go ahead.' That sounds like a railroad. But you could hardly say anything else, could you ? Oh, Louis, I am awfully in love."

" Little girl, you don't know what love is."

" Well, I like that. You ought to be ashamed of yourself to talk like that. Don't know what love is, indeed ! Is it love, when we are jealous of the trees and the sky, when one moment the heart is sailing toward heaven and the next in-

stant it is lying on the ground, almost dead with
anxiety? But wait till I tell you."

She told him her story and about her he put
his arm and kissed her. " Little girl, you do
know what love is—you know that it is the light
of the universe, the sun—God. And this outlaw
is to be your husband. But love itself is a divine
outlaw. It tramples upon reason. Man has
sought to regulate it, but he can not. The cynic
has striven to kill it with ridicule, but it has seized
the cynic and has made his soul beg for mercy.
God does not restrain it, for it is a part of Himself." And after a silence he added: " You say
that the Governor has pardoned him ?

" Oh, yes, and he isn't afraid to come in daylight now. He has talked with mother, and she
is charmed with him. He went to church with
me and everybody seemed to like him, and no
one here will suspect that he was ever anything
but a cotton merchant in New Orleans. Sappho
Block says that he is charming, and for the first
time I liked her."

" Who is Sappho Block ? "

" Oh, you know her — the Commodore's
daughter. But didn't mother tell you that she
had married a horse doctor ? I thought I wrote
about it, but I suppose not. She is married,

however, and the Commodore was awfully put out
at first, but he feels better now.   We arranged
for our wedding to take place immediately after
your return, and it shall be just as quiet as possible.   Of course there will be a number of people
at the house—we must invite our friends, you
know—but we don't want any display.   Oh, I
am so glad you don't object."

"I am not the censor of your heart, little one.
I have striven to be the governor of my own,
and have failed.   Will you tell me one thing,
Ellen: I ought not to ask it, but I must.   Do
you think that Rose loves me?"

"Why, Louis, you ought to know.   Can't you
see?"

"No, for I am blinder than a bat.   But let us
not talk about her.   Come, let us go to the
house."

"But, Louis, you don't seem to be interested
in my wedding."

"Oh, yes I am.   Wait and you shall see how
much."

"I am so glad to hear you say that.   And I
know that you will never say anything to wound
him, for you forgive everybody, don't you?"

"Almost everybody," he answered.   "But
let us go.   Mother is calling us."

She laughed and chattered as she hung upon his arm, but he was silent, and his heart, which he had thought lay dead, was fierce with life.

CHAPTER XXII.

Avery preached another narrow sermon, and again the intense and gloomy religionists heaped their congratulations upon him. An old woman cried out that she had seen the glory of the Lord, and to her wayward son she tottered, put her arms about him, and implored him to acknowledge the Master, to turn from the ways that were dragging him down; and with cold beads upon his brow the preacher stood, gazing vacantly at the scene.

The Commodore was charmed, and, lightly tiptoeing in his happiness, he made his way to Avery, and, leading him from a group of women and standing him up against a fence, thus declared himself: "I have been greatly bowed down, and therefore be it said that your words have elated and comforted me, for they teach me that this world is simply on the market, and will soon pass away. But I must have a few confidential words with you in order to complete my happiness. I'll liberate him in a moment," he added, turning to the women and bowing to

them. " I won't keep him long. I want to talk
to you," he went on, facing Avery, " and I seek
this semi-public opportunity, for I am not
ashamed of what I am going to say. But first
let me tell you how glad we are to welcome you
home. Swamp fever in one respect is like—I
might say, like love; it is an exacting master,
but I knew that you were stronger than the
fever, although you may not be stronger than
love."

" What is it you wish to say, Commodore ? "

" Yes, that's what I am getting at—what I
have intended to get at all along. There are
times, you know, when an old salt must talk,
when a sea-dog must bark, and I am tacking now,
but I'll sail up to my point pretty soon. I suppose you have heard of my daughter's marriage.
It bowed me down and slit my ears—marked me
like a hog with a crop off the left and a swallow-
fork in the right, but I am straightening up, and
soon I hope to be erect enough to look up at the
chickens as they go to roost. And you must now
pardon my bluntness, for I am a monster of the
deep, but what are your intentions toward Miss
Sibley ? There, I knew I was blunt, but an old
sea-horse—"

" You have said enough, Commodore. But

why should you suspect, sir, that I have any intentions toward her?"

"Now you embarrass me, my dearly beloved. I am sentimental and acutely sensitive even if I am sometimes referred to as a rip-snorter in business. But I am a shrewd discerner, and in my sly way I find out many things which, be it said, escape the less searching eye of the fatted calf, by which I mean the public. And drawn by my adroitness, and yet wholly unsuspected by the young person herself, has come the knowledge of her, let me say, estimate of you. To be blunt and therefore unavoidably personal, she thinks a great deal of you, and I earnestly hope and trust that your regard for her is such that—but your people are waiting for you and I will not detain you any longer. Good day; hope to see you again soon. And please pardon the uncouthness of a weather-beaten double decker that has seen too much service."

Mrs. Avery was happy and yet she was annoyed, for as she was walking toward home, leaning on her son's arm, she said: "Now, I'd like to know what right that impudent man had to take you off there and keep you so long when hundreds of people were anxious to tell you what they thought of the sermon. Rose, dear, why do you and Ellen walk so fast? We won't try to keep up with them, my son. Mrs. Marshall told me that she had never heard such a sermon in her life, and you know that she is from one of the very best families in the country, and she did want so much to tell you of the good it did her, but no, that man must take you away when he might have known how proud I was of you. What did he have to say that was so very important?"

"What he said really amounted to nothing, mother."

"But it must have amounted to something, my son, otherwise you would not have stood there so long. Had it anything to do with my failure to tell you that your salary had been forwarded to the mountains?"

"Nothing whatever."

"I didn't know but it had. Won't you please tell me now what made it of so much concern? How did I do wrong in keeping the money for you when you had told me to be as economical as possible?"

"Mother, at the proper time I will tell you everything."

Dinner was served under the arbor. The day was perfect; the air was delicious with a per-

fumed coolness; there was no glare of sky, but
the softened pink which in the gulf region comes
to fore-paint a change of season.

Ellen was happy, but Rose was depressed.
Avery asked her what had brought about her saddened mood, and she answered that she was not
feeling well; and hereupon Mrs. Avery spoke her
mind: " Well, of course, some people are some
way and some another, but as for me, I don't see
how any one could possibly feel bad after hear-
ing that sermon.   And I want to say that this is
not a mother's partiality; no, indeed, for it would
have impressed me just the same even if it had
been preached by an utter stranger."

" A sermon can be very poor medicine for the
body, mother, even though it might serve as a
tonic for the soul," Louis replied.

" That may be true, my son—I say it may
possibly be true—for I have reached that time of
life when we begin to think that it is wise to dispute nothing, but I must say that I don't see how
any one could possibly listen to that sermon
without being benefited both in soul and body."

" I don't think that my spirit was attuned to an
enjoyment of it," said Rose, sitting meditatively
with her elbow on the table and with her chin
resting in the palm of her hand.   " And yet all
along I felt glad that he was preaching it."

Mrs. Avery affectionately leaned toward her, "I am delighted to hear you say that, my child, for I don't mind telling you frankly that your gentle influence has had much to do with keeping my son in the straight orthodox pathway. Now, Louis, please don't say that she has not influenced you."

" No, mother, but I will say that she has."

Rose looked at him, into his eyes, and he put his hand to his brow and was silent; but the girl's mood was changed. "Oh," she said, "the withered bloom didn't fall this time, Mr. Louis, for all the blooms up there now are bright. I have thought of that withered flower so many times."

" And you must have thought of other flowers, too, for you put them on my dresser while I was away."

" Yes, Mr. Louis, for it was a pleasure to me."

" But you gathered them one day in the rain," Ellen spoke up, slily looking at her brother.

" Yes, but that was also a pleasure," Rose replied, smiling. "The day had been hot and the rain was cooling. And the next day, Mr. Louis, I went down the river in a canoe—went to see the vine cross."

" Did you ? And what did you think as you looked at it ?"

" I thought of many things—of our visit, and of the red breasted bird that seemed to be flying about with its heart exposed."

Mrs. Avery, looking over her shoulder, began to frown. " There is that same cow trying to open the gate. I wonder why people in this part of the country can't keep their wretched cows at home. Why, such a thing as a cow going about pestering the neighbors wouldn't be tolerated in the East. What were you going to say, my son ?"

" Nothing."

" But wasn't something said about a vine cross ? What about it ? I haven't seen it, I'm sure. And if it really amounts to so much, why hasn't something been said to me about it ? Is everything of importance to be kept from me ?"

" Oh, it is a mere fancy, mother."

" But am I not here to enjoy fancies as well as anyone else ? Has it come to the pass that a mother is to be denied the luxury of a fancy ? What about it ?"

" It is a beautiful cross formed of a dead tree and covered with vines," Rose answered; " and some day before long I will take you to it."

" Will you go to the cross before I go to the altar ?" Ellen asked, laughing. But her mother did not laugh.   The old lady's eyes filled with tears, and whimperingly she said:

" I don't see how you can speak so lightly on so serious a subject.   I couldn't, I'm sure.   Is marriage becoming so trifling a matter ?   I want to know ! Oh, I don't object to Mr. Haywood.   No, not in the least.   He is just as nice as he can be, but it does grieve me to give you up.   Oh, I know what you are going to say—you are going to say something about the cattle man and the other men I wanted you to marry, but I tell you that it is nothing more than natural that a mother should desire to see her daughter well settled in life.   But this has come on so suddenly that I haven't had time to think it over.   It is a great sacrifice when a mother is called upon to give up her child, that is, for a mother who has any heart. But we can simply live and do the best we can. Louis," she added, " it seems to me that you have again taken up that same look of distress; and you were so well when you came home.   I don't know what is to become of us all, I'm sure. But this is no time for questioning the wisdom of the Lord.   I have nursed my son through fever, and now I must prepare my daughter for marriage."

Evening came, and the roses that had nodded

at noon now opened their lips to drink the freshening dew. Avery walked down the river alone, and within his breast the same old combat was raging. His heart was a Lazarus, arisen from the dead, but not to find the soothing love of a Saviour, a healing balm, but again to take up a list of troubles, sorely, one by one. The questions which so many times he had asked himself, and which never had he answered, now were asked again. But there must be an end, perhaps a cure. He turned aside as if this thought lay near the river—-he strode far off into the darkening woods, but he came back to the water's edge and to the thought, and now it seemed to be floating on the water, in the moon-light. Again he turned aside, and this time he did not go back to the river; he went to the ruined summer house. And there, with shadows folded about her like a sable robe, stood Rose Sibley, looking upward, her hands clasped.

" Oh, is this you ?"

" Yes, Mr. Louis," she answered, stepping from the low heap of ashes, and standing under a fig-tree, facing him.

" But perhaps you want to be alone," he said, stepping upon the pile of ruins.

" I would rather be with you," she frankly replied.

" Surely you are out-spoken. Rose, be true to yourself, for then you are true to nature, and nature is true to God."

She looked up at him, and the moonlight caught her sad smile. " I do try, Mr. Louis—-I think I am truer than I appear. Standing where you are now, I was looking over the life I have lived since I came to this place. And it seems mostly to lie in this garden, with light and shade about it, now bright, now dark—but it must end —it is ending."

" No, it must not end!" he cried. " It shall not."

" Yes, it must. When Ellen goes, I shall go. Your mother refuses to take pay for my board. Yes, I must go."

" I told her not to accept another cent until fifty dollars are accounted for. But will you put this thought aside until after Ellen is married?"

" Yes, if you wish me to. I feel that I am a child, and that it is my duty to obey. You speak to me with the voice of my father; your eyes and your words are his."

He stood looking at her, struggling with himself. " But I don't want to appear as a father," he said. " You say that you must obey me. Is it out of reverence? But you must not answer that question.   And you will remain until Ellen is married ?"

" Yes, if you wish it."

" I do wish it—I demand it.   Tell me, has your life here been happy ?   Has a grief followed you—"

" I have been happy and miserable, Mr. Louis, but all my life I have been elated or depressed."

" Could I have made you happier ? "

Her hand lay upon a branch of the fig tree and the leaves were trembling.   " You have always done your duty, Mr. Louis.   Shall we go to the house ? "

CHAPTER XXIII.

Old Jude had raked the yard and the shrub-berry in front of the house had been trimmed. Horses pranced in the road and buggies drew up at the gate. Arm in arm, Avery and a tall, dark-haired man walked up and down the porch. The man laughed a great deal and Avery was smiling. Mrs. Avery was important and dignified, but at times she was tearful. She was about to see her daughter settled, and she was grieved to put aside a long-standing worry.

Among the guests were the Commodore, Sappho and her husband. The Mayor and the city councilmen came, with their linen coats glossily ironed. The Commodore, meeting a man whom he addressed as " Judge," said to him: " Let me see you a moment."

The " Judge " followed him to the fence. The Commodore, placing his hand on the top board, indeed, ripping off a splinter, putting it into his mouth and beginning to chew it, thus began to talk:

" I reckon you think I am the biggest liar hung

or unhung, and let me in humility acknowledge
that I have given you good and sufficient reason
to think so, but life is an old liar and is never so
happy as when she compels her children to lie.
I told you that I would repay that twenty-five
dollars and—"

" But, Adams, this is no time and no place to
speak of it."

" Under the circumstance, Judge, you are par-
donable for omitting the title, but I appeal from
your decision, sir. This is the place and the
time to speak of it. Debt has all times for its
own; and as I owe you, I am your slave. The
only human being I ever was afraid of is the
man I owe, my master. If you choose to put a
chain around my neck and lead me about these
grounds, I will submit with a Christian martyr's
humility. If you desire it, you may put me on
that stump and auction me off, and I will go
home with the highest bidder and black his boots
and clean out his well."

" Adams, you have passed my office every
day—"

" True, too true, in fact," the Commodore
broke in. " Yes, on trembling joints I have
passed your office, for fate, the heartless agent
of the lying world, branded me a liar and I was
afraid to stop. Get your chain."

"Adams, you are worrying over this affair much more than I am. The truth is I had forgotten the twenty-five dollars."

"Hah, speak softly, Judge. Oh, what is so generous as forgetfulness. Judge, there is a reciprocity between us, a charming affinity, for in truth, I had forgotten it myself. But I recall it most vividly now, and to-morrow morning, while the dew is yet on the stubbed grass, I will bow down before you with the money held up to you; but, Judge, in case I don't, stretch the tendons of a courtesy and forget it again for a day or two."

The "Judge" laughed. "Adams," said he, "you are a refreshing scoundrel."

"Judge, you wound me deeply, and while I am ready to forgive, I can not forget. Charming young lady about to be married, sir. Judge, you have a beautiful daughter. Tell her to marry a stick. A stick is the best husband. Wise men make women unhappy. My daughter married a stick and he adores her. Smart men look for flaws and find them. Smart women the same way, perhaps, but it is easier to blind their beautiful eyes. Here comes my daughter's stick. Doctor, you know the judge, don't you?"

The "Doctor" flipped his cap brim, ducked

his head, and remarked that he was glad to see the "Judge" in the race. "They are about to lead 'em out," he added. "May call 'em back, but we'd better be in at the first start."

Soft air was stirring and the roses were peeping through the garden fence. There had been the low buzz of subdued talk, and from the house laughter had come like a spiritualized echo, but now all was hushed. Then arose the solemn and measured words of an old man and then followed a rippling of forced merriment, of talk that was tearful but light. Mrs. Avery came out upon the porch with a handkerchief to her eyes, and following her came Louis, who gently led her back into the room. Now all was spirited, almost gay. Ellen was handsome and happy; the bridegroom was stately, but with many a humorous nod.

"You do look so sweet," said Sappho, speaking to the bride. "The doctor thinks you are charming, and he is such a character. You will like him when you know him better. We are awfully sorry to lose her, Mr. Haywood," she added, addressing the man whom the governor had pardoned; "but we know that you will take good care of her. Miss Rose, you look charming, too. We shall lose you next, no doubt. But before you go I want you to see my play.

read it to the doctor and he thinks it exquisite, don't you, dear?"

" Tap, tap."

" Now, isn't he a charming character ? So laconic. And here's father, smiling on you. I know Mr. Haywood must soon learn to like him."

The Commodore warmly shook hands with Haywood. " We are delighted that you should have formed so close and so charming an alliance with our growing town," said he. " But you have plucked one of our sweetest flowers. It's all right, however; it's business."

." Oh, father, how can you ?" Sappho cried.

" My daughter, I entreat your pardon. Lately I have been simply a money changer, turning the temple of sentiment into a commercial den of thieves. Ah, and here is the judge." And then in a whisper he added: " To-morrow while the dew is still on the stubbed grass I will greet you with willing money in my outstretched hand."

The guests were gone, the family sat in the parlor. On the morrow Ellen was to leave her home. The first shadow of evening fell across the doorway. The bridegroom was laughing. " Louis," said he, " you may tell them a story."

" Do, brother," Ellen cried. " You haven't told one in so long."

" I am not much of a story teller," Avery replied, " but I feel that on the present occasion
something is due from me, and therefore I shall
make an attempt at—I was going to say fiction.
But Ellen, will you promise not to say a word
until I am done ? "

" But why must I promise that ? I hate to
promise a thing and not know what it's for. You
haven't asked Rose to promise."

" We can rely on her. I simply want *you* to
promise."

" Well, that's complimentary, I'm sure. But
I promise. Go on with your story."

" And not an exclamation shall escape you ? "

" Now, what on earth do you mean ? Yes, I
promise even that."

" Well, put your hand over your mouth. Here
we go. One time there were two boys at college. They were sworn friends, just as two girls
might have been, but when their school days
were over they lost sight of each other, just as
two girls are almost bound to do. One day,
many years later, they met again. It was at a
large gathering on a river. They hugged each
other. They talked nonsense and wondered why
they had never written to each other.

" 'Oh,' said one, 'look at that girl over there,

the one with the pink fan.   She entrances me—
I am in love with her.'

" 'She is my sister.'

" 'The deuce you say!   Introduce me.'

" 'You say you are in love with her?'

" 'Yes, desperately.   Who could help loving
her?   I have always loved her—have been looking for her.'

" 'She is my sister.'

" 'The deuce you say!   Introduce me.'

" 'To introduce you would kill the romance.
That is, unless you are a poet.   Can you write
poetry?'

" 'It's as much as I can do to read it.'

" 'Then, my dear Andrew, your case is hopeless.   You are in business, you tell me.   She
hates a business man.   She is the most foolishly
romantic creature alive.'

" 'But will you let me win her?'

" 'You can't.   Numerous men have tried.'

" 'But I can.   I have a new idea, romantic
enough to be winning.   I will be a robber and
let her reform me.   I—' "

Ellen sprang from her seat.   "Oh, you think
you are awfully smart, don't you.   But it's
nothing for you to laugh at.   It's a shame, that's
what it is.   I don't like to be deceived that way.

I haven't deserved such treatment.   I don't like
it at all.   And mother, did you know it all
along?"

"Louis told me in the mountains."

"Well, I don't care, you all think you are
awfully smart.   But I will pay you, sir," she
added, putting her arms about Haywood's
neck.   "You think you are so cute, but let me
tell you that I would have loved you even if I
had found you selling bacon in a swamp, pad-
dling about in a dug-out canoe.   So, there!"

CHAPTER XXIV.

CONCLUSION.

At daylight a carriage called for Haywood and his wife, and when the vehicle had rolled away, Avery turned toward the river and slowly strolled along the dewy path. No intention measured the distance he was to walk; his stroll was aimless; his vacant look was cast upon the ground. The sun came and flashed behind him and in front of him the dew-drops gleamed, but he saw nothing, heard nothing save the ringing tumult within his own breast, and he felt that now it was fainter, slowly dying. Surely the end was near, for on this day he was to tell her to go or beg her to stay. But could he bid her stay? Should he press her to his bosom to draw the sorrow out of his heart? After all, would it not be a soreness healed by a poison which in its turn must inflict a deeper and a deadlier wound? But surely the combat was fainter, the struggle weaker.

He lifted his heavy head when the pathway dipped down into an oozy place, and looking

about him, found that he was opposite the lily bed.
The sunlight fell upon the marsh and glorified it.
The light fell also upon other places, but to him
it seemed that the marsh had caught the smile
of God. He heard a boatman rowing, saw a
man coming towards him.

"Set me over and wait until I come out of the
woods!" he cried.

The man gazed at him, letting his boat drift

"Did you hear what I said?"

The man plied his oars and the boat touched
the shore.

Avery stepped into the boat. "Row me
straight across and wait for me no matter
how long I am gone."

The man said nothing. "Did you hear me?"
The man nodded.

Avery leaped upon the shore and hastened
straightway toward the vine cross. Once more
would he pray for counsel, for help, and if it
should be denied him—he sprang aside as if to
avoid the company of such a thought.

The cross, protected from the earliest rays of
the sun, was dripping with dew; and upon his
knees the preacher sank and mingled his tears
with the tears of the morning. He looked
upward, and there at the arm-ends of the cross

were the red blooms—the blood of the Son of
Man. He groaned aloud and his agonized sup-
plication died away tremulous in the forest.

"Holy God!" he cried, throwing himself upon
his breast, "I know not which way to turn.
Call my tortured soul, even if it be to send
it blackened into torment, for any misery, O
God, would be a relief from this. Why are Thy
creatures endowed with the power to make one
another so wretched, O Saviour of man, whom I
have almost forgotten—"

Into the damp grass he pressed his face,
sobbing: "O, I have forgotten Thee, I see Thee
not, and this hell is my punishment."

The sun was above the trees and the warm
light fell upon him. His eyes were dry and the
tears of the morning had ceased to fall. A long
time he lay there, and then he sprang up with the
cry:

"*She shall not go!*"

Back toward the river he went, now running,
now dragging his feet. He glanced at the sun.
Hours had passed since he fell at the foot of the
cross. But the boatman was waiting for him.

"Row me over."

The man took up his oars, but said nothing.
And Avery spoke not a word until he stepped
upon the shore, and then he asked:

"What do I owe you?"

The man answered not, but held up four fingers.

"What do you mean by that? Four dollars?"

The fellow nodded, and Avery tossed him the money. "You are a robber," he said; "but you are of the world and the world is a thief. But why don't you speak? Can't you talk?"

"Yes, and mighty loud at times."

"Scoundrel!" Avery shouted, shaking his fist at him. "Wolf, I know you, and I ought to have cut your throat."

"Ah, hah, and will you be ready for me on the fifteenth? Say, wish I hadn't made such an easy bargain with you. And by the way, I'm pressed this month and must have a hundred or I spout. But when I come I will bring a man with me."

Avery did not reply, did not look at him as the boat drifted away.

At the garden fence the preacher halted. He climbed the fence, he picked his way to the ashen spot whereon the summer house had stood, and here he dropped upon his knees. This he knew was his last resistance, weak, feeble. Suddenly he sprang to his feet, trembling, almost choking. A sweet voice was singing, and he heard the piano, swept by a passionate hand. It was over —the struggle was ended. Slowly he walked

toward the house, and into the parlor he stepped just as the music ceased. Rose, sitting on the piano stool, turned toward him.

"Don't say a word," he said, slowly advancing. "Don't speak a word until I have told you something."

Her face was bright with a new smile, a smile he had never seen before. "I will do as you bid me, Mr. Louis."

He stood with his arms folded. She sat looking at him with a tender glow in her eyes.

"Woman, never was human being loved as you are loved. Woman, I know your dreadful story. I have stood on the spot where you murdered a man; I have cast myself upon the floor in the room where the girl binds up the leg of the wounded stork—I have bought off the damnable law, meeting its agent in the garden, giving him fifty dollars at a time toward the settlement of the five hundred reward offered by a governor. I know that a man wronged you— there, don't turn away—I know that a man deceived you and that you killed him; I know that the man was my brother—but, O God, woman, I worship you and your love is all that can draw the deadening pain out of my heart. Oh, to me, even with blood on your hands, you are an angel, and I bow down in idolatry before you."

At her feet he dropped upon his knees. and she caught his head in her arms and pressed it upon her lap.

" Oh," she sobbed, and her tears fell upon his hair; " oh, a love like this can atone for a world of misery.   Louis, my darling, my precious, listen to me.   I will tell it as calmly as I can.   A man swore that if I would not marry him he would kill himself.   I could not love him—I told him I could not—but, day after day, he swore that unless I would agree to marry him he would kill himself.   A woman loved him and hated me, and whenever he came near me I always sought her; I could not listen to his pleading, it distressed me so.   One day I was in the parlor, sitting at the piano.   He came in, and the wild look in his eyes frightened me—almost hypnotized me with fear. He walked up to me and touched my hand with a pistol, and before I could move, before I could scream, so stupefied was I with fright, he turned the pistol upon himself—fell dead.   At this instant Georgia Morton rushed into the room, shrieking, and I heard her cry, ' I saw you murder him and you shall hang for it.'"

She was silent for a moment.   Avery looked up at her, sprang to his feet, pressed her to his heart.   Again he knelt upon the floor. with her hands pressed to his face.

" You must let me tell you," she said. " I was frightened, I was weak, I thought I couldn't explain—in a flash I saw a judge and a court-room—disgrace—and I ran away, I hardly know how, and hid myself. I knew that the woman would swear against me, my mind was so weakened by fright that I could fancy anything, and I didn't know but that she might really believe I killed him, and even when I became more sensible I was afraid to go back. I thought of a jail and crowds of people staring at me. For weeks an old woman kept me secreted in her house—a woman whom my father had befriended. The newspapers called me a murderess. I couldn't give myself up after that, so I stole away with the old woman's aid, I hardly know how; and at last I came here, after wandering about, and I would have told you everything, but I was so hungry for your love, and I was afraid you would not believe me. Only one person in Denver knew where I was—the old woman—and just now I received a letter from her—here it is—enclosed with a confession and a letter from Georgia Morton. A strange preacher went to Denver and preached directly to her, she says, and her heart melted and she sought the forgiveness of Christ. Here is the letter, precious, and here are the cuttings from the newspapers, telling of the great crime against me."

In his arms he caught her, to his easing heart he pressed her, and together they sank upon their knees, with their eyes turned upward, silent; and the vine at the window was whispering.

[THE END.]

www.ingramcontent.com/pod-product-compliance
Lightning Source LLC
Chambersburg PA
CBHW030758020726
47499CB00006B/1676